Rock Island P
401 - 19th Stre
Rock Island, IL 61201-8143

W9-BLG-271

-- NUV 2012

ZEUGLODON

ZEUGLODON

The True Adventures of
Kathleen Perkins, Cryptozoologist

by James P. Blaylock

SUBTERRANEAN PRESS 2012

Zeuglodon Copyright © 2012
by James P. Blaylock.
All rights reserved.

Dust jacket illustration
Copyright © 2012 by Jon Foster.
All rights reserved.

Interior design Copyright © 2012
by Desert Isle Design, LLC.
All rights reserved.

First Edition

ISBN
978-1-59606-454-6

Subterranean Press
PO Box 190106
Burton, MI 48519

www.subterraneanpress.com

For Kathy, Perry, and Krysta Rodriguez,
Secret Members of the Guild of St. George

And, as ever, for Viki, John, and Danny

Acknowledgements

I'm happy to thank a number of people who read this book in its early stages and made sensible and encouraging suggestions or lent me needed inspiration: Paul Buchanan, Heather Buchanan, John Blaylock, Lew Shiner, Tim Powers, Karen Fowler, and our old friends Sue and Barry Watts of the St. John's Lodge in Bowness-on-Windermere, England.

I first began writing *Zeuglodon* as a sort of illustration for the students in my Origins and Sources of Fiction class at the Orange County High School of the Arts, so they're largely to blame for its existence. By now they've all gone out to make their way in the wide world, but perhaps the stuff of this book (if they ever run across it) will call up pleasant memories.

Finally, in the writing of this novel I owe an enormous debt of gratitude to a number of luminous books (and the authors who wrote them), many of which books my mother encouraged me to read at an impressionable age, thus sealing my fate as a certain sort of writer: *Journey to the Center of the Earth*, *Twenty Thousand Leagues Under the Sea*, *The Mysterious Island*, *At the Earth's Core*, *Pellucidar*, *The Return of Sherlock Holmes*, *Huckleberry Finn*, Edith Nesbit's *The Treasure Seekers*, and the seafaring novels of Howard Pease.

"We shall pick up an existence by its frogs. If there is an underlying oneness of all things, it does not matter where we begin, whether with stars, or laws of supply and demand, or frogs, or Napoleon Bonaparte.
One measures a circle, beginning anywhere."

Charles Fort
Lo!

Chapter 1

The Day that Three Things Happened

How it all started was like this. Brendan, Perry, and I were taking Hasbro for a walk one foggy morning last spring, because Brendan claimed he saw a mermaid on the rocks at Lighthouse Beach. He had said things like this before, telling us one time how he had seen a gigantic octopus tentacle come up out of the kelp, and then another time a pterodactyl eating fish on the rocks. The pterodactyl had turned out to be a big pelican, which was better than the octopus, which turned out to be a figment.

Brendan was hanging onto the leash and Hasbro was pulling him along toward Mrs. Hoover's house. Hasbro is part bulldog, you see, and he's very strong, and there's no holding him back if he's anxious to be walking. He's kind of fat, too, although Uncle Hedge says he's actually just portly, which is a pleasant way of saying fat, and there's no reason not to be polite around dogs as well as around people. I could see Mrs. Hoover working in her front garden, in among the roses. She's our neighbor three doors down, and a very nice neighbor, too, as you'll see. There was a woman talking to her, a tall, thin woman, who looked sort of picklish and who was writing in a notebook. We didn't know it then, but the woman was Ms Henrietta Peckworthy, who is a member of a very troublesome do-gooder society. Ms Peckworthy was about to become our nemesis, our soon-to-be-sworn-enemy.

What happened was that Hasbro spotted Mrs. Hoover's Persian cat, whose name is Pete and whose face is entirely flat. Hasbro followed Pete along the edge of the bushes toward the Hoover backyard, pulling Brendan with him. Pete started running, and when Hasbro tried to chase him he yanked Brendan over onto his face in the wet grass and got away into the fog, which was very thick now. Perry ran after Hasbro, and I bent over to help Brendan up. It was just then, when both of us were hidden by fog and bushes, that I overheard Ms Peckworthy talking.

"No rules at all is what they tell me," she said to Mrs. Hoover. "A steady diet of doughnuts and ice cream. Up at all hours and roaming the bluffs and beaches. I understand that the small boy tumbled down the side of the cliff and broke his arm."

"That would be Brendan," Mrs. Hoover said. "Boys will be boys."

"I daresay they will, if they're allowed to be. And that poor little girl with no mother to look after her. A perfect little tomboy. Her aunt is *very* worried about her. Toliver Hedgepeth might mean well enough, but he's an eccentric of the first water, and he's no kind of parent for three impressionable children."

That was me, the "perfect little tomboy." And John Toliver Hedgepeth is our Uncle Hedge. Who is the aunt that's so very worried about us, you ask?—Aunt Ricketts, who lives in Los Angeles and shoves her nose into everyone else's business, because it's a very long nose. We're not fond of Aunt Ricketts.

"And the small boy will no doubt fail in school this year," Ms Peckworthy was saying. "No doubt at all."

I saw that Brendan was boiling mad now, because there really was *some* doubt, although not a lot. Ms Peckworthy was obviously a treacherous informer and spy, and that's the thing that Brendan hates most in the world.

Perry was coming back with Hasbro now, and I motioned for him to keep hidden, and so he ducked down and crawled toward us across the lawn, hanging onto Hasbro's leash with his teeth. Unlike Brendan, Hasbro was in a very happy frame of mind, and his head, which is large, was bobbing from side to side, like one of those dashboard dogs with his head on a spring. I was afraid that he was going to start barking, which he often does when he's happy. So I shook my head at him and gave him a hard look.

"Mrs. Ricketts intends only to do what's right for the children," Ms Peckworthy was saying now. "She would hate to bring Social Services into the matter, but there's the children's welfare to think about. I fully intend to take them back to Los Angeles when I return south at the end of the week. I'll leave my card with you."

"That's as may be," Mrs. Hoover said boldly, "but I don't care a rap about your Mrs. Ricketts and what she wants. I've never heard of the woman."

Ms Peckworthy started up again. I don't know what-all she said, because I was thinking about that last terrible thing: "...take them back to Los Angeles." If she had said that the world was going to explode at the end of the week it wouldn't have been nearly so bad. Without my having a chance to stop him, Brendan stood up, put his thumbs in his ears, and waggled his fingers at her while sticking his tongue out and squinching up his eyes. He often does this to show contempt.

Ms Peckworthy was apparently astonished to see him, popping up out of nowhere like this, looming through the fog and making faces. I stood up, too, and Ms Peckworthy stepped backward and put up her hands as if we were going to leap over the bushes and attack her. Before I could say anything useful, Pete the cat appeared on the lawn behind her, having come all the way around the house. Hasbro made a dash at Pete straight through the bushes, and Ms Peckworthy stepped back onto his leash, which was coming along like a snake. Somehow she fell over backward and said, "Oh! Oh! Oh!" Mrs. Hoover went to help her and so did Perry, except that Ms Peckworthy shouted, "Assassin!" and wouldn't let Perry near her but acted as if he meant to harm her.

She crawled to her feet, picked up the little notebook, shook it at us, and walked off very quickly without saying another word, looking back over her shoulder with her pickle face. She got into her tiny red car and drove away. So ended the first awful appearance of Henrietta Peckworthy.

That wasn't the end of anything else, though, not by a long sea mile, as our old friend Captain Sodbury would say. Brendan wanted to get down to Lighthouse Beach in order to find his mermaid before the fog got any thicker, and so we forgot about Ms Peckworthy, said goodbye to Mrs. Hoover, and pursued our course along the bluffs, with me minding Hasbro now. The sea path runs right along the edge of the cliffs, with the ocean breaking on the rocks two hundred feet below, and it can be dangerous in the fog, especially with the cliffs all crumbly after last winter's rain. Brendan hurried on ahead, but I shouted at him to slow down, because the fog was getting heavier all the time. And sure enough, very soon the fog closed behind him like a gray curtain, so thick that we couldn't tell right from left except for the sound of the ocean away below us and the grumble of trucks out on the Coast Road.

After a moment the fog swirled on the sea breeze, clearing just a little, and we spotted Brendan up ahead, standing still at the end of a dirt road that comes down from the highway. He wasn't alone. There was a car parked there, turned around and facing back out. A man stood beside it. The car door was open, and the motor was running. Steam was coming up from the exhaust pipes, mingling with the fog, and you could see the taillights glowing red like the eyes of a deep-sea fish. There was no license plate on the car. It was then, at the worst time ever, that I realized I'd forgotten my evidence camera. I *never* forget my evidence camera, but now I had, and there was no going back for it.

"Krikey," Perry said in a low voice, "I believe it's the legendary Lord Wheyface the Creeper." He pointed with his walking stick, a piece of driftwood that he had found on the beach and dubbed "the Melmoth Walker," which made no more sense than calling the stranger "Lord Wheyface the Creeper." That's Perry's brainy way of being funny. Some people find it obscure.

The man was very pale, almost the color of the fog, and he was tall, with long scraggly black hair and a hooked nose. He wore a worn out velvet trench coat with gold buttons, like a gypsy or a pirate would wear, and a pair of heavy black boots and tight-fitting black gloves. He had the look of someone who was from someplace else, and a not very pleasant place, either. He waved at us in a way that was meant to look friendly, but there was nothing friendly about him, especially his smile, which must have been surprised to find itself on his face because it didn't seem to want to stay there.

"I've lost my little dog," he said in a wheedling voice when we came closer. He looked around at the empty bluffs, shaking his head sadly. "His name is…Bucket."

"Bucket?" Perry said. "What kind of dog?"

"A Shih Tzu," he said, pronouncing it wrong, although I won't say how. He cupped his hands to his mouth and shouted, "Bucket!" out toward the ocean, shaking his head sadly. "Bucky-boy!"

"It's pronounced '*shid*-zoo,'" Perry told him.

"Of course it is, the poor little thing. She's no bigger than that." He held his hands together now, indicating that the dog was maybe the size of a tuna can. "You've got a dog yourself," the Creeper said, gesturing at Hasbro. "You understand how sad I feel. I thought maybe the four of us could find little Bucket easier than I could by myself, alone in all this fog." He waved roundabout himself at the empty bluffs.

"The four of us?" Perry asked him shrewdly. "How did you know how many of us there were? Some of us were hidden in the fog until just a moment ago. You must have thought there was only one of us and not four."

"I could hear your footsteps," he said. "I counted them and divided by two."

"Except that we have ten legs," Perry said shrewdly, "because one of us is a dog. You must have thought there were *five* of us."

"I'll tell you what I *thought*," the Creeper said, sounding very nasty all of a sudden. Then he tried to smile again, but his smile was rickety, like a broken thing. "Smart lad," he said. "You remind me of myself, when I was your age. A ready answer for.... *Oh my heavens what's that!*"

We all looked in the direction he pointed, and in that instant he leapt forward and snatched at Brendan, who shouted and sort of back-pedaled, falling over a rock, which was lucky, because the Creeper would have had him for sure instead of empty air. Hasbro sprang forward, and I let go of the leash, and in two seconds Hasbro had gotten hold of the Creeper's boot with his teeth. The Creeper edged toward

Brendan again, hauling Hasbro with him and shouting, "Get off! Get off!"

Perry ran past me, raising the Melmoth Walker over his head with both hands and slamming it down on the Creeper's shoulder hard enough to snap the stick in two. The Creeper reeled backward, clutching at his shoulder, with Hasbro still clamped onto his boot.

"You filthy little...!" he started to say, and he moved menacingly toward Perry now, dragging Hasbro like a ball and chain. Perry raised the broken-off piece of stick and stepped back a pace, just as Brendan sprang to his feet and ran for it, darting past the Creeper and straight down the path toward home, shouting for Uncle Hedge.

"Run!" Perry hollered, and I did, and so did Perry. We ran as fast as we could while Hasbro held onto the Creeper's boot long enough for us to get away. Then Hasbro let loose and tore out after us, still barking, and passing us like a meteor. Through the fog I saw Mrs. Hoover's back fence looming ahead, and I thought we were safe, but when I looked back again the Creeper was, running hard, scary close. But his heavy coat billowed out behind him, slowing him down like a parachute, and his boots were real clompers. I heard a grunt and an unpleasant shout, and I looked back again to see that he had fallen flat. He got up, looked in our direction, and turned around, limping back toward his car in a hurry. In about ten seconds Uncle Hedge appeared, just in time to get a good look at the man's back before the fog rolled in again, hiding the bluffs and the Creeper and the Creeper's car.

When we came in through the kitchen door, Uncle Hedge dialed the police in Fort Bragg, talking to his friend Captain Smith, who knew a little bit about Uncle Hedge and his "work" with the Guild of St. George, which I'll tell you about later. We met him twenty minutes later at the end of the road back out on the bluffs, although now there was nothing of the Creeper left to see except tire tracks. Of course we described him as best we could, but none of us could tell Captain Smith about his car, except that it was old and green, and in the fog it was hard to say whether it wasn't maybe more gray than green or the other way around. It had no license plate, of course, so we told him that much, but Captain Smith said, "He'll have put it back on by now," meaning that the Creeper had taken if off on purpose, so that didn't help much either. What *would* have helped? It would have helped if I had brought my camera. But I didn't, and it was nothing but spilt milk under the bridge.

Captain Smith took a picture of the tire tracks and boot prints, but there wasn't much else to do. He told us that it was unlikely we would see the Creeper again, because he was a conspicuous stranger, and now it wasn't safe for him in Caspar, not lurking around dressed like that. And anyway, he told us, we were "a tough crowd," and had probably put the fear into him. Then he gave us a lecture about talking to strangers. The story of the little dog was a lie, which of course we had known all along, and so we were fools to listen to it for even a moment.

"Run first," Captain Smith told us, "and ask questions later."

By now the fog was so heavy that the air was wet, and none of us were in the mood to go on down to the beach to look for Brendan's mermaid, even if Uncle Hedge had let us, which he didn't. He said it was a good day for staying inside while he tried to sort things out.

"We need to have a confab," Uncle Hedge told us when we were back in the kitchen eating a bowl of Weetabix with bananas. He looked very grim, which isn't usual for him, and so when he *is* grim you pay attention. "There's more to this

Creeper fellow than meets the eye," he said. "I want you to give him a wide berth. Keep your eyes peeled for the man, and if you see him again, try to make sure he doesn't see you. Call me or call Captain Smith. He won't try to trick you next time. He'll strike, and quickly, too."

"Who is he?" Brendan asked.

Uncle Hedge sat there silently for a moment, poking at his soggy Weetabix with a spoon, before saying, "I've seen him once before, and heard of him a couple of times, but there's a great deal about him that I don't know. I've got my suspicions. But even if I *did* know what he was up to, that wouldn't protect us from him. We'll have to use our wits for that. Confronting the man out on the bluffs today was witless. I'll tell you that straight out. You've got to use your heads for something besides hat racks."

◪

A little while later—and this was the third bad thing of the day—a man named Mr. Asquith came out from Social Services and talked with Uncle Hedge and with Mrs. Hoover about the "attack," as Ms Peckworthy had reported it (and that's how we found out her name). Mrs. Hoover said it was all a lot of malarkey, that it wasn't any kind of attack at all, and that Ms Peckworthy was a busybody who had tripped over her own feet. Then she said nice things about the three of us (leaving out Brendan's making rude gestures) and about Uncle Hedge and Hasbro. Mr. Asquith nodded and said he was glad to hear it. Then he said he was parched, and he drank a glass of water in our kitchen where he chatted more with Uncle Hedge, although we were sent into the other room. Before he drove away he patted Hasbro on the top of the head and called him "old son," which Hasbro very much appreciated. It seemed to me that Mr. Asquith was way too pleasant to take sides with someone like Ms Peckworthy.

But after Mr. Asquith left, Uncle Hedge called us together for another confab. He told us that we must take Ms Peckworthy very seriously, and not do anything that she could write down in her notebook. Thank goodness, he said, that she didn't know about our run-in with the Creeper, because that was just the sort of thing that Aunt Ricketts would seize upon to prove that we were living in an unsafe environment. We didn't want another visit from Mr. Asquith, Uncle Hedge told us, no matter how nice he seemed to be. He said this in a way that made even Brendan look worried.

Chapter 2

Uncle Hedgepeth,
the Guild of St. George,
and the Rest of Us

It was Perry's suggestion that I start this story with rousing action, which is what I tried to do. He says a reader wants some excitement right off, but I say that although that might be true, it's both necessary and polite to introduce oneself, and that's what I'm going to do now, because so far I've mostly neglected it. You already know about Hasbro, who like I said has some bulldog in him and several other noble things. You also know something about Ms Peckworthy and Aunt Ricketts, although the less you know about Aunt Ricketts the better. I wish *I* knew less about her.

At first I thought maybe I should let Perry write all this down, because besides being my cousin, he's a writer and I'm not. I'm a scientist, although the science teacher at my school, Mr. Collier, says I have too much imagination, but that I might be a scientist when I grow up and forget what I think I know. I say that if a person forgets what she thinks she knows, it's hardly worth growing up at all. Mr. Collier called that "Peter Pantheism," but I don't believe in isms, even if they involve Peter Pan.

My name is Kathleen, which is an Irish name. Uncle Hedge calls me Kath sometimes, but mostly he calls me Perkins, which is what Perry and Brendan call me, too, and it's the name I prefer. I'm eleven years old and I'm what is called a cryptozoologist, which is a scientist who studies legendary animals, although the only reason they're legendary is that they don't appear very often. But how often does a comet appear? Most of the time it's out wandering around in space, which is the same with so-called legendary animals, which wander around in the ocean, or in the high mountains, or in some other very distant and lonesome place, like Scotland, and you can hardly blame them. That's why I carry the evidence camera. You never know when a giant octopus or a mermaid is going to rise up out of the ocean.

What do I look like, you ask? I'm not very tall, and I have dark hair that I keep short because it's easy. I have brown eyes, and although Brendan won't admit it, I'm taller than he is, if you measure carefully and he doesn't cheat. And I'm older too, by more than a year. In three months I'll be twelve, and he'll still be ten, which seems to bother him. But he's young, and so maybe he's sensitive. Brendan was named after the great Irish navigator who came to America in a small boat with nothing but a telescope and a fishing pole and who is now a Saint. (I'll tell you more about Brendan some other time, when he's not looking over my shoulder to see what I'm writing down, which is rude if it goes on for very long, which it very definitely has.)

I was named after Kathleen Ricketts, who is also our Aunt Ricketts. Sometimes I wish I were named after Joan of Arc instead. When Joan of Arc went off to war, someone said very rudely that she should stay home to cook and sew, and she told them that there were already plenty of women to cook and spin, which showed a great deal of spirit. Of course later they burned her at the stake, but probably not just because of her comment about cooking and spinning.

Just so you know, Perry is tall, especially for his age, which is thirteen. He's already as tall as Uncle Hedge, and very skinny. He has dark hair that falls into his eyes and makes it seem like he's peering at everything. He reminds me of Sherlock Holmes in the old movies, even his nose, except he doesn't smoke a pipe and he doesn't wear one of those coming-and-going hats.

The town we live in is called Caspar, which you pronounce like the name of the friendly ghost. It's near the city of Fort Bragg in northern California. Caspar can be a lonesome place, especially in winter. When I look out my bedroom window, down toward the Sea Cove, there's nothing but ocean for eleven thousand miles, and then you run into Japan, which is another thing that some people thought was legendary until three Portuguese sailors washed up on the beach in a storm and "discovered" it.

Our great Uncle Hedgepeth is our mothers' uncle. Perry and Brendan don't have the same mother as me, but our mothers had the same uncle because they were sisters, and that uncle is Uncle Hedge. Uncle Hedge has a sister, too, and that's Aunt Ricketts. Perry and Brendan are orphans.

I'm not an orphan, although my father died very young—too young for me to remember him. I live with Uncle Hedge because my mother, Abigail Perkins, is missing. When her deep sea submersible vanished in the Sargasso Sea two years ago, she was searching for the oceanic tunnel that connects our own Atlantic Ocean with the ancient ocean that lies within the land at the center of the hollow earth. If you've read Jules Verne or Edgar Rice Burroughs (who called the land Pellucidar) you've heard of it. Probably you think it's a made up place, but I know for a fact that it's not. My mother's submersible was never found, and the scientific research vessel that took her to the Sargasso Sea sank with all hands, although nobody knows how or why or quite where, because the Sargasso Sea is vast and empty and is a place where strange and cryptic things occur.

I don't talk about what happened to my mother, because when I do, people get a sort of frozen stare on their faces, like they've been petrified. I wrote a paper about the interior world for my science class after reading a book called *The Hollow Earth* by Dr. Raymond Bernard. The book is a scientific account of Admiral Richard Byrd's discovery of the polar opening to the interior world, and about his finding warm water currents flowing out of that world into the icy water of the Arctic and Antarctic oceans, carrying flowers and seeds and the leaves of extinct species of trees. Mr. Collier said that the book was a barrel of half-baked baloney, but for a cryptozoologist like me it's very interesting indeed, no matter how much it's baked.

You can believe in Pellucidar or not, and I won't blame you if you don't. But like I said before, no one believed in Japan, either, until they got there, and then there they were. Uncle Hedge worries when I talk about my mother still being alive, partly because he blames himself that she's gone, and partly because he thinks I'm getting my hopes up and will only be disappointed. But I think that *up* is the only place to get your hopes, because otherwise they're not hopes.

There are two things I have to tell you about Uncle Hedge, and both of them are actually *very* strange. One thing is that he's the caretaker of the Secret Museum near Glass Beach in Fort Bragg. It's a museum that's a kind of warehouse rather than the kind of museum you buy a ticket to, and it's full of odd and unlikely things, which you'll learn about very soon. Another thing is that John Toliver Hedgepeth is one of the secret geniuses of the world. And I don't mean that he's one of the secret *smart* people of the world when I say that. I mean genius like in "evil genius" except that Uncle Hedge is one of the good sort, unlike Professor Moriarity or Fu Manchu or Dr. Hilario Frosticos, or other infamous bad people who have their vile fingers in every variety of crime. (The word "vile" spells "evil" if you mix the letters around. Perry pointed this out, and is writing a codebook of significant words.) The thing is, you don't as often hear about the good geniuses as you do the evil ones, and even if you did hear about the good ones you wouldn't know whether they were merely very good and very smart both together, or whether they were some other kind of thing.

That's what John Toliver Hedgepeth is—some other kind of thing. And he isn't the only one. They're a kind of secret society, except Uncle Hedge doesn't really keep it a secret, because no one believes it anyway, which he says is way better than a secret. They call themselves the Guild of St. George, after George of Merry England, who famously killed the dragon and slew the necromancer Ormadine and became one of the Seven Champions of Christendom. It's the Guild that actually owns the Secret Museum. Uncle Hedge's able assistant is Old Sally, who lives at the museum and is our great good friend. Who is Dr. Hilario Frosticos, you ask? He's the nemesis of the Guild of St. George, but I don't want to talk about him until I absolutely have to.

Uncle Hedge didn't tell us about his being a secret genius, by the way, because that would be too much like bragging. Mr. Vegeley told us. Mr. Cyrus Vegeley owns the Albion Doughnut Shop out on the Coast Highway in Caspar. Believe it or not, it's a haunted doughnut shop, although that doesn't figure into this story, and so I'm not going to mention it. Its address is number 13, which is one of the three significant numbers, especially if something is haunted, and which might or might not be a coincidence depending on whether you believe in coincidences. I mostly don't.

Later that afternoon, when Mr. Asquith left, we drove down to the Albion and ate doughnuts, because Uncle Hedge said that we wanted a little something to "put us back on our feet." And that's where the next chapter starts, with the Principal Characters eating doughnuts at the Albion Doughnut Shop, Number 13, The Coast Road, Caspar, California, on the very far edge of the Western World.

Chapter 3

What Happened
at the Secret Museum

I remember it was four in the afternoon, which Uncle Hedge calls "the doughnut hour" after the famous poem by Henry Wadsworth Longfellow, whose middle name sounds like bubblegum if you've got a really lot of it in your mouth. We drove down to the Albion in Uncle Hedge's Cadillac Coupe de Ville, which is very old, and which has tremendous long fins in the back. You can't really call it a "car" which is too small a word. Uncle Hedge calls it "the vehicle," and Mr. Vegeley calls it "the rig." We three call it the "Zeuglodon," which you pronounce like zoo, but with a glow-don attached to it. Zeuglodons were enormous sea creatures that supposedly died out during the Cretaceous period, many millions of years ago, although I have my suspicions about that. We have the bones of one in the Secret Museum.

The Zeuglodon automobile is a sort of watery blue, with balloon-like white-wall tires. Uncle Hedge keeps it ferociously clean. One time when it got a dent in it Mr. Vegeley popped the dent back out with a plumber's helper, the rubber kind you use to unplug sinks. It left a big round mark that wouldn't wash off. Perry and I told Brendan it was from the tentacle of a giant octopus, which maybe gave Brendan "ideas," as they say, since he's been seeing giant octopi ever since.

We were the only ones in the doughnut shop besides Mr. Vegeley, who is always in the doughnut shop unless he's not. He serves doughnuts in little plastic baskets, pink, blue, or yellow, with a sheet of waxed paper. It's all very decorative. Mr. Vegeley calls glazed doughnuts "the true quill" and he often quotes an old Irish saying that goes, "A plain glazed doughnut is your only man," which Brendan finds confusing despite his illustrious namesake having been Irish. By late in the afternoon, the sugar on the outside of the glazed doughnuts has hardened into little sheets, like crisp paper, and it's really very good—so good that it was hard to pay attention to Brendan, who was yammering on about what he calls his "general theory of navigation," telling us that he's never in his life been lost, because direction is perfectly simple. North, he was telling us, is always straight ahead. That's how St. Brendan the Navigator found North America and why sailors follow the North Star. If they follow the North Star they always get there, wherever it is, and it's naturally always straight ahead. But I pointed out to him that if you're at the North Pole, standing right on top of it, and you start from there, then *south* is always straight ahead and north is always behind you, which makes a sad mockery of his theory of navigation. What Brendan knows about navigation you can put in your hat, and Perry was just telling him he could put it there when the phone rang, which it hardly ever does at a doughnut shop.

Mr. Vegeley said "Uh huh" three times and then hung up the phone, looking worried and untying his apron. "It's Old Sally," he said to Uncle Hedge. "Someone's broken into the museum."

"She's not hurt?" Uncle Hedge asked anxiously, but already he was out of his chair and heading for the door.

Mr. Vegeley was switching around the "Open" sign so that it became a "Closed" sign, and was saying that Old Sally wasn't hurt, but had been locked into the kitchen by the intruder and had just now gotten free. Outside we climbed into the Zeuglodon, with Hasbro sitting on the back seat with the three of us, and we drove away hell for leather toward Glass Beach and the Secret Museum. (I borrowed that phrase from Perry. I don't really know what "hell for leather" means besides fast, and neither does Perry.)

The sky was cloudy now from a storm coming in off the ocean, which had blown the remnants of the morning fog away. The clouds were moving along very low on the sea wind, and the ocean was dark and rough and streaked with foam. Glass Beach is on the north side of Fort Bragg, nearly to Pudding Creek. You turn left past the Skunk Train and past the lumber mill and hundreds of stacks of piled up lumber to where the road turns to dirt. The museum is in a big open field on your right. It's made of gray wood, the color of fog, and it looks like a warehouse, which in fact it was, back in the old days. Behind the museum, all the way down to the cliffs above Glass Beach, there's another open field, although it's not really "open," because it's over your head in mustard weeds and berry vines, so thick that unless you know about the tunnels that go through it you can't get across it at all, but have to take the Glass Beach Trail. We drove up to the museum just as it was starting to rain hard. Old Sally was standing out front waiting for us, holding an open umbrella and looking large and irritable. She's got what is sometimes called a "rough-and-ready" face.

"He's gone into the shrubbery," she said at once, pointing into the field.

"What did he look like?" Uncle Hedge asked her, but she said she didn't know for absolute certain. She had only seen his shadow when he slipped up on her unawares and shut her into the kitchen. Then he had pushed something against the door, done his dirty work, and gone out again, the stinking pig. She had seen only his dark shadow ducking away into the field. He was carrying something—almost certainly one of the exhibit cases. But she couldn't be sure what it was, and the Secret Museum is full of exhibit cases.

Uncle Hedge told the three of us to "stay out of trouble," and then he and Mr. Vegeley headed down the open trail toward Glass Beach. The tunnel through the vegetation leads that same way, and once the man came out of the tunnel and onto the beach they would have him trapped. Because of the surf and the rocks at the top end of the beach, he couldn't get away to the north, and unless he meant to swim for it he would have to come back down the beach toward the trail and the lumberyards at the south end in order to escape, and there they'd have him. We went inside the museum with Old Sally to look for clues, although Old Sally wasn't interested in clues, but wanted to put on a pot of coffee.

It was shadowy inside the museum even though the lamps were on and even though what was left of the day was still coming in through skylights in the high ceiling. There was the sound of rain on the roof as we walked up and down the aisles between the exhibits, which are sort of frozen, staring back at you from behind dusty glass. Some of them are stuffed and some of them are floating in alcohol or formaldehyde, and some of them are boxed up in crates so that you can't see them at all. The first thing you notice, because you can see it from everywhere, is the skeleton of the zeuglodon—not Uncle Hedgepeth's car, but a real zeuglodon skeleton, sort of, that's eighty feet long and looks like a giant sea serpent. Its toothy, long head is way up by one of the skylights in the ceiling, and its long neck curves down and down into its body, which is shaped like a narrow egg, if you can imagine that, but an egg with flippers. It was the terror of the seas back in the Mesozoic era. All of it is just bones, of course. Silver wires hold it to the ceiling. I said it was a *sort of* real skeleton because actually it was made out of pieces of *four* skeletons that were dug up in Arkansas a long time ago by the charlatan Dr. Albert Koch, who fastened four sets of neck bones together to fool people into thinking it was a very long sea serpent and not a zeuglodon at all. Here's what's funny: when people found out that they were being fooled, they didn't care, but came to see it anyway, and *paid* to see it, which is another thing that goes to show you.

Anyway, almost as soon as we started looking for clues, Brendan shouted that the Hopkinsville Goblin was missing. But it wasn't. Brendan was in the wrong aisle. The goblin was in its glass case next to the mummified Mayan Princess and the Fish Eye Array, which is two dozen glass globes with fishes' eyeballs floating inside. The biggest is a whale's eye that's as big as your head, and the smallest is the eye of a gummidgefish, which you can't even see without an immense magnifying glass, and even then it might just be a speck of dust on the lens.

"*Concentrate*," Perry said. "What would a thief break into the museum to steal?"

Before anything came into my mind, Brendan shouted, "Thomas Edison!" and we all rushed over to the cabinet with Thomas Edison's last breath inside. His breath isn't just floating around in the cabinet. It's in a jar with a twist-on lid that's very old and a little rusty and with wax melted around the edge of the lid to seal it so that the breath doesn't escape. Henry Ford himself captured it in the jar when Mr. Edison expired (which means died and which also means breathed, which I think is very interesting indeed). Henry Ford was famous for inventing the assembly line, which Uncle Hedge says is one of the most famous of all the lines, including the equator, although he says it's inferior to the chorus line. When Mr. Edison died he was in the middle of building a spirit telephone that would allow you to talk to dead people. It worked, too, except nobody knew the number, or at least that's what Uncle Hedge told us. The spirit telephone is in the museum, too, and some day we're going to crank it up and see who answers.

Thomas Edison's last breath was still in the jar, or at least the jar was still in the cabinet and the lid was still waxed onto it. The spirit telephone was next to it in a glass box, safe and sound. We went on down the aisle and right away we saw what *was* gone. It was the Feejee Mermaid, which is in a sealed box made out of glass and wood. I don't mean the fake mermaid that P.T. Barnum the circus man had, which was sewn up out of monkeys and carp skin, but the *real* Feejee Mermaid, which washed up out onto a South Seas island in a storm and dried out in the sun until she was the color of a coconut and had shrunk down to about three feet tall.

Perry found a footprint in the dust, and he went back after the gummidgefish magnifying glass in order to detectify it. Brendan and Hasbro went off to look around the rest of the exhibits to see whether anything else was gone. But it would have taken both hands to carry off the Mermaid, and so I didn't think that the thief could have stolen anything else, not if he was escaping on foot. I went to ask Old Sally whether the Mermaid had maybe been put somewhere else and hadn't been stolen at all. Old Sally said that the Mermaid must have been what the thief was carrying when he ran, the filthy scoundrel, because the box was just that size.

I went back into the museum where right away I ran into Perry acting suspiciously. There's a workroom off the hallway that's about as big as someone's garage, with lumber in it and sheets of glass and tools and cans of paint. It has a wooden floor that's kind of beat up and stained, with a piece of carpet in the middle of it. Perry was standing in the hallway, leaning over and looking in through the open door. He turned and waved at me to hurry, and he put his finger to his lips. When I looked past him, I saw right off that the window was pushed wide open. The cold wind that was blowing in smelled like rain, and the floor was wet around it, and there were muddy footprints leading from the window to a place in the middle of the floor where the rug had been hauled back and a trap door was standing open.

I didn't need a magnifying glass to figure out what had happened. The thief hadn't gone down to the beach at all, but had stowed the mermaid somewhere and come in through the window to finish the job. Perry made a pushing gesture, meaning the trapdoor, and I nodded. We tiptoed forward like Hansel and Gretel sneaking up on the witch, listening to the shuffling and scraping under the floor. We were very nearly close enough when suddenly we saw a hand come out, and we stopped dead. The rest of him was hidden by the open door, so he couldn't have seen us yet, although maybe he heard our footsteps on the floorboards. Very slowly he peered past the edge of the door straight at us. It was Lord Wheyface the Creeper, and the look on his face was poisonous.

Chapter 4

Out Through the Window

Perry leaped forward and threw himself against the door, which slammed down, knocking the Creeper back into the hole but banging against his wrist and hand and not closing all the way. We heard him shout, a really angry shout, and Perry tried to kick his hand back under the edge of the door so we could get it down flat and trap him. The hand twisted and caught Perry's ankle, and Perry tripped and fell away from the trap door with the Creeper still holding onto him. I jumped for it, pushing hard against it, but it was no use, and the door opened hard and threw me backward. Brendan ran in, goggled at us, and ran back out just as the Creeper let go of Perry, tossed an old leather briefcase out of the hole and onto the floor, and hauled himself out. Perry scrambled away, and the Creeper clambered to his feet and bent over to snatch up the briefcase.

Run first, I told myself, but before I could take a step he lunged straight at me. I screamed and tried to twist aside, but quick as a snake he grabbed me by the jacket, then threw his arm around my waist and started dragging me back toward the window. I screamed again and thrashed around, but he held on tight, and I just knew that he was going to drag me right out through the window, and so I started kicking and flailing my arms around and hitting him with my elbows, and if I could have got to him, I would have bitten him, too.

Perry rushed forward like a hero and tried to grab the briefcase that the Creeper was holding onto, but the Creeper fought him off with his free hand, with Perry bobbing back and forth, and all the time we were backing up toward the window. Old Sally ran into the room clutching a broom and looking as much like an army as any single person can look. Brendan followed behind her, carrying the gummidgefish globe with both hands like he was going to smash the man with it. Then Hasbro dashed in, barking like a mad thing, but very confused and distracted by the hole in the floor until he saw that it was the Creeper who was causing the problem and went after his boot again. Old Sally slammed the Creeper with the broom right on the side of the head, and he grunted and jerked back. My feet left the floor as he picked me up to shield himself from the broom, shouting, "Stop!" so loud that everyone *did* stop, including Hasbro.

Brendan was holding the gummidgefish globe over his head, and Old Sally gripped her broom like a spear. Perry was breathing hard and kind of shaky. Nobody could do anything without hurting me, or without the Creeper hurting me. He shuffled backward a couple of steps, carrying me even closer to the open window. He pitched the briefcase backward out into the rain, and for an awful moment I thought he was going to throw me out the window too. Instead he sort of twisted me around and stared at me. I hoped to never see a face like that again, it was so mean and ugly and hateful.

"Mark my words," he said in an evil way, "I'll know you again, pillbug," and he dropped me onto the floor right then and there and slid out through the window quick as a wink. Old Sally threw the broom, though, and it hit him square in the back, and although he jerked a little and grunted, it didn't stop him. He picked up the briefcase and ran along the side of the museum in a downpour of rain, heading toward the ocean. Perry grabbed the gummidgefish globe out of Brendan's hands, because it looked like Brendan was going to throw it through the window, just out of excitement. If it broke, the invisible gummidgefish eye would have been lost forever in the weeds, because it's very nearly impossible to find an invisible eye once it's gotten lost.

Old Sally helped me up, and we headed straight out of the workroom and toward the front door of the museum, just as it swung open and Uncle Hedge and Mr. Vegeley came in, a minute too late. One good thing, though—they were carrying the Feejee Mermaid, safe and sound.

"He came back!" Old Sally shouted at them, and she pointed in the direction he had gone just moments before. Mr. Vegeley set down the Mermaid and both of them turned straightaway and went back out into the rain toward the tunnel, moving wonderfully fast for their size. We followed behind them now, Hasbro, too, because nobody had time to tell us not to, and we plunged right into the tunnel with Uncle Hedge leading the way.

The first thing we did was slow down, because it was dark in among the vines and mustard plants, with only a little daylight showing through. The farther we got down the tunnel, the darker it became. It was still kind of dry in there despite the rain, which shows you how thick the vegetation was. You had to stick right to the center, because if you got over to the side of the tunnel, the thorns on the berry vines would scrape you. As it was they kept snatching at my hair and jacket.

"This is no good," Uncle Hedge said, stopping at last. He looked behind him and was surprised to see us. "You children go back. Now," he said. He wasn't smiling when he said this, and we turned around and started back like he told us. I didn't mind, because the rainwater had started dripping from the tangle of vines overhead now, and was running down my neck and the back of my jacket, and the tunnel smelled like old moldy leaves and other discarded things.

I was glad to get back to the museum kitchen, where the heater was going, although as soon as I got in and was safe, the strangest thing happened. I started shaking all over and then started to cry, because I couldn't help it. It was as if I could feel the Creeper's arm around me and see his face again. Brendan and Perry told me it was all right to cry, and so did Old Sally, who poured hot cocoa for us and found some cookies in the larder, as she calls the pantry, and pretty soon I was all right again.

In about ten minutes Uncle Hedge and Mr. Vegeley came back empty-handed. They hadn't caught the Creeper, who had probably doubled back up the Glass Beach trail and gone into the lumberyards. Old Sally poured cups of coffee for the two of them and then poured one for herself, and Uncle Hedge had us tell him the story from the beginning—how Perry had hear suspicious noises, which led him to the work-room, and how he and I had tried to imprison the Creeper by closing the trap door, but had failed.

"So he took the briefcase!" Uncle Hedge said when I got to that part. For some reason he didn't seem unhappy about it, which was strange, although it wasn't something that I paid attention to at the moment. "And the three of you!" he said, looking narrowly at us. "I believe I told you to stay out of trouble, and here you were attacking this Creeper fellow with your bare hands. He might have hurt you just because you had gotten in his way, and nothing served by it either."

"We didn't know who he was," I said, "and we didn't *want* to fight with him." It sounded like a lame excuse, because it was.

"It was very brave of you," Uncle Hedge said in a kindly way. "And I honor you for it, but it was the wrong thing to do. It was an IQ test, and you two failed it. I believe a possum could have passed it. I'll remind you that Ms Peckworthy would take a dim view if one of you were to be knocked on the head or carried away. Let *me* attend to the man, if he needs attending to. Probably he's long gone by now, and with any luck he'll keep going."

"What was that thing he stole?" Brendan asked. "That old briefcase?"

Uncle Hedge thought for a minute, as if he were making up his mind whether to tell us or not, because maybe it was too dangerous to tell us. I could see that he didn't want us mixed up in this thing at all, whatever it was. But then because we were *already* mixed up in it, he *did* tell us, and this is what he said: the Creeper had stolen some hand-written journals—the journals of a man named Basil Peach, a member of the Guild of St. George, and an adventurer and explorer. Peach's explorations took him to far-flung parts of the world, and he made maps of secret places, which he drew right into the journals. Some of his maps charted openings into the land at the center of the Earth, and it was one of those maps that had led my mother into the depths of the Sargasso Sea, never to return. The Feejee Mermaid belonged to Basil's ancient father, Cardigan Peach.

Uncle Hedge hadn't seen Basil Peach for a long time, nearly twenty years, and during that time the Mermaid and the briefcase with the maps and journal had been stored in the Secret Museum for safe keeping, except it turned out not to be all that safe after all. The Creeper wanted the very two things in the museum that were the rightful property of the Peach family. But why? That was the unanswered question. There was a silver lining to the whole thing though.

Uncle Hedge had removed the most important maps from the journals back when my mother made her fateful trip to the Sargasso, and he kept them locked up safe at home. The Creeper thought he had the maps, you see, but he didn't, or at least he didn't have the ones that mattered.

By the time we left the museum, taking the Mermaid with us, it was dark. The rain had stopped, but the night was cold and the sky was full of tearing clouds, with the moon appearing and then disappearing behind them. When we turned up the Coast Road, past the Skunk Train Station, what should I see parked in the lot but a tiny red car with someone sitting inside. "Ms Peckworthy!" I said, and everyone looked, and sure enough it *was* her, alone in the dark car, waiting.

But waiting for what? Or perhaps for whom? We drove along in silence, and I couldn't help but wonder whether the Creeper had gone out of our lives now that he had gotten the briefcase, or whether he had been drawn more deeply into them. "Mark my words," he had told me. "I'll know you again." The memory of it made me shudder, and I had to force myself to think about other things.

Chapter 5

The Black Iron Key

That night after dinner we were eating vanilla ice cream with chocolate syrup in the kitchen. Uncle Hedge let us dish it out, because it had been a long day, and we had four scoops apiece in big bowls with so much chocolate syrup that there was a chocolate lake in the bottom. Brendan said the lake was a tar pit and the scoops of ice cream were the sinking bodies of albino wooly mammoths, but he had only just thought this up when Uncle Hedge cleared his throat in a meaningful way. We forgot about the mammoths and the tar pits because he looked serious and thoughtful.

"You recall Mr. Asquith?" he said, and of course all of us did.

"I think he was nice," Brendan said.

"That he was," Uncle Hedge said, "and lucky for us that he *was* nice. This business at the Museum has set me thinking, though." He took off his spectacles and polished them on the tail of his shirt, and then he held them up and looked through them before putting them back on. I could see that he was trying to think up the right words to say, as if they were important words, but even so I was surprised at what he said next.

"Ms Peckworthy has something important to tell us," he said, "and I want all of us to listen to her."

"*Peckworthy*!" Brendan said, snorting it out through his nose.

Uncle Hedge held up his hand and shook his head. "Never you mind her for the moment. What I mean to say is that... is that I've tried to be a father to you three, and maybe sometimes I haven't done as good a job as I might have."

Immediately we all shouted that he had too, but he waved us quiet and went on. "Sometimes a man is good at being a father because there's a good mother alongside of him."

"There's Old Sally," Brendan put in.

"And we're lucky to have her. But she's not a mother, is she? And I'm not a father," he said, "not really, although I do what I can."

He drew in a deep breath and fell silent for a moment. Old Sally had told me once that our mothers were the daughters that Uncle Hedge never had, although now he's got me, which I hope makes up for it a little bit. Perry and Brendan were very quiet now, and I was, too, because I was thinking about my mother, just like they were probably thinking of their mother, and I knew that Uncle Hedge was at least partly right. It didn't matter to me that Ms Peckworthy had called me a perfect little tomboy, because of sticks and stones and all that, but there were times, a lot of times, when I wished I could talk to my mother, if only for a few minutes, to ask her things that I couldn't ask Uncle Hedge. It was hard right then not to cry, but I didn't, because I knew that Uncle Hedge felt bad enough, and I didn't want to make it worse for him. If *he* started to cry it would just be too awful.

"What I mean to say," Uncle Hedge told us, "is that we can't let Ms Peckworthy be right."

"She's *not* right," Brendan said. "I'm doing better in school. I did my history paper on John Adams and what's-his-name, the other Adams, and I did my leaf collection, and

I did extra credit for science, too. We proved that thing about hot air, didn't we, Perry? With the balloon in the oven?"

"Charles's Law," Perry said. "Gas volume and temperature."

"That had an explosive result, as I recall," Uncle Hedge said. He didn't add that it also had a stinking result when the burst balloon glued itself onto the floor of the oven.

"That's what proved it," Brendan said proudly. "I wrote up a hypothesis and everything, and even a graph with the explosion at the end of the line. I used colored pencils."

"Very scientific of you," Uncle Hedge said. "But we've got to be sure that we aren't failing any classes, or even coming near it. Do you understand me, Brendan?"

Brendan poked at his melting wooly mammoth and nodded his head.

"And we won't trouble Ms Peckworthy with nonsense of any other variety? Or give her any other sort of evidence to cudgel us with?"

"No, sir," Perry said, and I said it, too, and so did Brendan, although Brendan didn't look sure about it, and I knew it would be necessary for Perry and I to take him aside and threaten him, because if Brendan turned out to be the weak link, it would be curtains for all of us, curtains being Aunt Ricketts.

"Your parents would be very proud of you," Uncle Hedge said after a moment. "And you can be very proud of them." It seemed as if he wanted to go on and explain what he meant, but he didn't because he saw that there wasn't any need to. Some hard things needn't be said at all, when everyone already knows them. Uncle Hedge said he had work to do then, and he went off toward his study, which is very like a library, full of old books of every sort and with maps and sea charts on the wall and mementos from distant lands cluttering the shelves.

We went back to our ice cream, but I couldn't concentrate on it, because I was thinking about my mother, and because the Mermaid was sitting right in front of me on the kitchen table, looking out through the window into the darkness. And it *was* dark outside. If there was a moon in the sky it stayed hidden, and every now and then raindrops pattered against the window. There was a flicker of lightning, too, out over the ocean, although it must have been very distant, because there was no thunder to be heard, at least not yet. It was a good night to be inside the house eating ice cream where it was warm and dry.

I began to wonder what language the Mermaid had spoken when she was alive—maybe some kind of bubble language—and whether she had a mother and a father and a kitchen to eat ice cream in, or whatever mermaids eat. Her bottom part was a tail, exactly like you would imagine, with big scales about the size of nickels, and the kitchen light shone on them so that they reflected little rainbows that were really quite pretty. The Mermaid herself must have been much prettier, too, before the sun poached her. Her eyes were made of glass, but they twinkled as I imagined her eyes must have twinkled long ago, and she seemed to be gazing into the Great Beyond, maybe recalling her life in the Sargasso Sea and longing for her final resting place.

Perry sat at the table staring closely at the Mermaid's box, as if he was studying things out. The bottom of the box was built of strips of wood that appeared to be glued together to make a board, and had been carved with the likeness of a moon and clouds on all four sides, with the tops of palm trees below the moon like a tropical island. There was the same sort of carving on each side, except that the moon was in different phases, with an old moon in front, very round and full, and a new moon on the fourth side, not even visible at all, but just a dark circle hidden by the shadow of the Earth.

Perry started fiddling with the edge of the box, where the strips of wood came together like little interlocking fingers. "It's loose," he said, frowning. "These pieces of wood are loose."

"Then leave it alone," Brendan told him. "You'll break it. Then what would you say to Uncle Hedge? He's already suffered enough."

"*You'll* be the one to suffer if you don't keep your opinions to yourself," Perry said. Right then he gave one of the wooden strips a push, and it moved a little bit, like the side of a Chinese puzzle box. It was the strip with the moon carved on it.

"*Now* look what you've done," Brendan said. "If you break the hermit seal and the air gets in the Mermaid will turn to dust."

"I don't think it's called a 'hermit seal,'" I told Brendan. But Brendan wasn't listening anyway, and neither was Perry, because the moon on the opposite side of the box had moved too, just a fraction of an inch, and *that*, I can tell you, was very exciting. Perry glanced up with the greedy look he gets when he's made a discovery, and we all crowded around the table to have a better view. There was a lightning flash just then, with a crash of thunder this time. Normally I love a lightning storm, but right now I scarcely noticed it.

Perry pushed on the opposite moon piece, and it slid open a quarter inch, which allowed him to push the first strip farther, too, and then a third one after that. One panel locked the other in place, you see, and when he pushed the two opposites apart, that unlocked the other two, and then he could push those apart, and when he did, the moon on all four sides of the box moved across the night sky above the palm trees.

"Let me try," Brendan said, but right then a sound started up from within the box, a curious sound, like a hive full of metal bees. There was a heavy click, and then a sort of ratchet noise, and the Mermaid herself began to rotate. We all stepped back from the table with our eyes wide open. She made one complete turn and then stopped, looking out the window again just as she had been. Weirdly, the strips of wood began to move on their own now, one after another, opening and shutting and opening again with more little clicking and whirring noises, until three of the sides ended up shut. The bottom front of the box remained open, though, and we could see that it was hollow inside.

Perry bent over to look, and just then the Mermaid began to turn slowly away from us again so that she was looking at the wall, and as she turned, the oddest thing happened. An immense skeletal hand reached out from inside the box, twice as big as a normal hand and with the bones fastened together with wire. The fingers were closed up, and within them lay a large, black iron key. The hand slowly began to open, as if to allow us to take the key if we wanted it. I wasn't at all sure that we did. Brendan reached for it, but Perry stopped him.

"It might be a trap," he said. "It might grab you."

The idea of it was just too horrible, and we all stood there staring at the hand, waiting for it to do something further. But it was apparently waiting for us, too, and perhaps had been waiting for a long, long time.

"It's like our jail keys," Brendan whispered, meaning the three iron keys that were in the toy box upstairs. And he was partly right, because the jail keys are also rusty looking and very large and heavy. But this was older, like a key that opens a pirate's treasure chest and has been buried in the sand for centuries, and it had little wavy designs carved into it, and when you looked at it you knew that it had to be the key to *something*, and not just any something.

Brendan started yelling for Uncle Hedge, and ran off toward the study to fetch him, and when they returned Uncle Hedge stood staring just like we did. After a moment, he reached out his own hand and carefully took the key. The skeleton hand closed and slid backward into the box. The Mermaid swiveled around to face us again, and one by one the strips of wood began opening and shutting, whirring and clicking, until the box was shut up tight and looked to be just as solid as it had been.

"I'll be a monkey's uncle," Uncle Hedge said, which was what he often said when he was mystified. "I believe this is a skeleton key."

"For a *very* big skeleton," Brendan said.

"You were clever to figure it out," Uncle Hedge said to Perry. "This key might prove to be crucial."

I could see that Brendan was irritated that Uncle Hedge had said Perry was clever and not him, because Brendan prides himself on being clever. And now I'd best reveal something about Brendan. He's kind of a glory pig, perhaps because he's young. Also he was still a little bit angry with us because we made fun of his theory of navigation, and he very much likes to be right and for us to be agreeable. When he wants to be right but we won't let him, he becomes really quite *sure* that he's right, and when that happens he convinces himself to do something foolish in order to *show* everybody. That's the mood he was in right now. I could see it in his eyes, which were frowny.

"Teach me how to work the box," Uncle Hedge said, and he watched closely as Perry pushed and pulled on the little strips. The box began to whir and make its ratcheting noises again, and Uncle Hedge said, "A clockwork mechanism!" to himself, just as the strips began to open and shut and the Mermaid turned around, and the hand slid out, and the fingers opened again, and the box fell silent.

"Perkins shall have the honor," Uncle Hedge said, and he handed the key to me. I set it back on the hand, exactly as it had been, and immediately everything reversed itself. The hand closed on the key and drew back into the box, and the box went through all its complications and noises until it was closed up and done and the Mermaid was gazing out the window as if nothing at all had happened.

Just then Brendan shouted and trod back into the edge of the table, staring hard at the rainy window and gulping air like a goldfish. We all turned to look, and for a split second I saw what Brendan had seen—a pale face ducking away outside the window.

There was the sound of footfalls—someone running down the drive and into the back yard, heading for the bluffs. Uncle Hedge strode toward the back door with all of us following, and he turned on the backyard lights in time for us to see the gate swinging shut but nothing else except the rain and the darkness. Perry said we should "give chase," but Uncle Hedge wouldn't hear of it. "Did you get a good look at him?" he asked Brendan, after shutting and bolting the door.

"It wasn't a *him*," Brendan said, looking more amazed than anything else. "It was a *her*."

"What *her*?" Perry asked.

Brendan stared for another moment and then said in a sort of whisper, "It was the mermaid from Lighthouse Beach!"

Chapter 6

Troubled Sleep

From my bedroom window that night I could see the bluffs above the Sea Cove, and the path winding along until it disappeared downhill toward the ocean. My mind was certain that the Creeper was somewhere out there in the shadows, watching our house. I tried to believe it had been Brendan's mermaid at the window, but I couldn't. I didn't believe in Brendan's mermaid at all. It occurred to me that Ms Peckworthy might be out there too, haunting the neighborhood, waiting patiently for the end of the week when she would load us into her tiny red car and take us away. Rain beat against the roof on and off, and there was the sound of water running in the gutters. When the rain dwindled away I could hear waves breaking in the cove and the moaning of the wind under the eaves of the house. I tried hard to sleep, but it was no use, and the time passed slowly.

I started thinking about how deep the ocean is and how lonely it must be for a mermaid who has gotten lost and been washed away by deep sea currents. I pictured the dark waters and the strange fish that swim there, and by and by I must have fallen asleep, because I began to dream about the Mermaid down among the waterweeds and fishes. In my dream she was in a bedroom of her own beneath the sea, with a bed made of pearls and shells. Then suddenly it was me in the underwater bedroom, and my mother was sitting at the foot of my bed, with the waterweeds moving behind her in the current. She spoke to me, and she reached out and took my hand in her hand, and I remember that I was *very* happy.

When I tried to say something to her I actually *did* speak, right out loud, and the sound of my own voice woke me from the dream. I can't tell you how sad it was waking up and finding her gone, because I don't quite know how to tell it. The thing about sleep is that people you've lost can come back to you in dreams. When you awaken they'll be gone all over again, but you know that some dark night they'll return when you really need them to, and you can speak with them again.

I lay there looking at the darkness, trying to recall the dream before it faded from my mind. By and by I saw a light go on out in the hallway. For a moment it shone like a yellow ribbon beneath the closed door. Then it went out again, leaving things even darker than they had been. I sat up in bed and listened. Hasbro wasn't barking, so whoever was out there was one of us. I waited for the stair tread to creak halfway down, but it didn't, which meant it wasn't Uncle Hedge. It was someone being stealthy. I waited a little longer, listening for him to return, but he didn't return, and that made me *very* suspicious indeed, so I climbed out of bed and peeked out into the hallway. The living room downstairs was dark, but I could see that there was a light glowing in the back of the kitchen, probably the pantry lamp, which would just be enough to lighten the breakfast nook, where the kitchen table was. And where the Mermaid was.

Halfway down the stairs I stepped carefully over the creaky tread and then went on down to the landing, where I stopped and listened again, hearing the ratchety sound of the Mermaid's box. I sneaked up to the kitchen door, and it was right then, when I bent down and looked in sideways, that I sneezed. Brendan (it was him at the kitchen table) jumped about half a mile into the air and he jammed both hands into the pockets of his pajamas as he spun around and gaped at me.

He had the very Face of Guilt, like an illustration in a book, and for a moment he made fish lips at me as he tried to speak. The Mermaid's box was open or nearly open. I could see that the little finger-pieces of wood had been worked away from the sides, but that was all I could make out before he stepped in front of it, looking as if he had just eaten something ghastly.

"*You better not tell!*" was the first thing he said. (Actually, he says that a little too often, although Perry and I wouldn't tell on him anyway. We're not rats.)

"I won't," I said. "But what are you doing?"

"*Doing?*" he asked. "What's *that* supposed to mean? I'm not *doing* anything. I just wanted my turn to open it. *Perry* got to open it. Nobody *let* him, he just *did* it. And now when I do it, it's a big crime."

"Nobody said it's a crime," I said. "I just asked what you were doing."

"And I told you I'm just having a look at the box, but now you've *spoiled* it!" He turned his back on me and started pushing the puzzle part of the box back together again, and the Mermaid turned around once, and the box shut itself up, and in a moment you couldn't tell anybody had been meddling with it. "*There*," he said. "I suppose you're *happy* that you've spoiled it."

"I didn't spoil anything," I said. "I just saw a light on and came down here."

"Well you *did* spoil it, and you'll have to live with that." He walked past me looking very dignified and headed toward the stairs. "Forever and *ever*," he said.

"I'll try," I said to his back. It wasn't clever. You never think of the really clever things till later. I switched off the light in the pantry and went back up to my bedroom, taking one last look out at the empty bluffs and the moon on the ocean before I lay down and fell asleep. The next thing I knew, the light was on and Perry was shaking me awake.

"It's *her*," he said, nodding hard over his shoulder. "The mermaid Brendan saw at the Sea Cove? *She's in the living-room right now!*"

Chapter 7

The Unexpected Guest

I followed Perry down the hall toward the stairs, with Brendan coming out of the bedroom behind us, rubbing the sleep out of his eyes. "What's the fuss?" he asked.

"There's mermaids afoot," Perry said, and Brendan said, "ha, ha, ha," very ironically, but by then we could see downstairs into the livingroom, and there she sat, in Uncle Hedge's big stuffed chair, spritzing herself with what looked like a perfume atomizer.

"*Seawater,*" Perry whispered.

She was short, so short that her feet didn't reach the ground. (I mean when she sat in a chair.) I don't really know how to describe her skin, but it was so white that it was almost a pale green that reminded you of the ocean. And she had gills, too, or something like them. You could see them low on her neck (although you tried not to stare—unless you were Brendan). They weren't flappy things, like a fish's gills, but were more like scars, maybe, the same on each side, and not useful. (Perry said they were called "vestigial" but of course he didn't say that until later. It's not the sort of thing you say in the presence of someone who's part mermaid.) Her hands were webbed like a frog's hands. You couldn't really see how much until she opened her fingers, which is just what she did when she gave me a little wave, because I guess I was kind of gaping at her and not saying anything, which isn't manners.

"I'd like to introduce Eulalie Peach," Uncle Hedge told us. "Her friends call her Lala. She's my old friend Basil's granddaughter, and she's come to us all the way from Lake Windermere. It's quite a surprise."

We all said how do you do, but we were too curious to be sociable yet. She was wearing a raggedy orphan dress and shoes that looked more like ballet slippers than proper shoes. They were black with orange embroidered koi goldfish on the toes, like the cloth shoes you see in Chinatown shops. Her hair was a little bit wild, because she had just come in out of the wind, and she had taken off her coat and dropped it onto the rug next to a worn out carpetbag made of tapestry material. She had flown into San Francisco and then taken a Greyhound bus up the coast, she said, which had left her off at the bus stop near the Albion, and she had walked up from there.

All of this made me highly suspicious, partly because she had a look on her face as if she thought everything was just a little bit funny, but also because Brendan had told us that he had seen her twice before, the first time being yesterday morning. I hadn't believed him, like I said, except now here she was, and so Brendan must have been telling the truth, because it's *way* too coincidental that he made up a lot of nonsense about a mermaid and then the nonsense had come true. All of us must have been thinking this same thing, even Uncle Hedge, but Uncle Hedge seemed happy to see her, and so I tried to put away my suspicions and be happy to see her, too.

What was she doing on our doorstep? She wanted to warn us about the Creeper, she said (although she described him, she didn't call him that) who had come out to this part of the world in order to steal something that belonged to her family, and he mustn't be allowed to.

"He already *did* steal it, just yesterday," Brendan said. "At least he tried to."

"Tried?" she asked him anxiously. "Then she's safe? The mermaid?"

Brendan told her yes, she was safe, and that we had beaten the Creeper witless with all manner of weapons and he had fled into the shrubbery.

"The other one...?" she asked, looking at Uncle Hedge now. He shook his head, and Lala looked relieved, but what it all meant I couldn't say. Now I know that she meant Dr. Frosticos, whose name she couldn't bring herself to utter.

We all went into the kitchen to make breakfast then, where the Mermaid still sat on the table. (Perry said that I should spell the Mermaid in the box with a capital M, because it was *the* mermaid, and had no other name. Lala must remain the lower case mermaid, because she does have a name, and by now we were getting used to it.) Anyway, Lala had come a long way to see the Mermaid, and she looked immensely relieved. It was awkward, actually, because no one wanted to say, "Are you related to this Mermaid in the box? You have gills and frog hands, after all," although we were all thinking it. Uncle Hedge started mixing up buckwheat pancakes, and pancakes are a good distraction, because eating gives you something to do besides talk. While we were spreading peanut butter on them, dipping them in syrup, and stuffing them down, she stole glances in the Mermaid's direction, as if she was trying to puzzle something out, and I wondered what it was.

I could see that Brendan was a little bit googly about her. He wasn't eating his pancakes, but was showing off and telling her about navigation and the north star and about how everything in the world is actually made of hydrogen, and she was nodding and saying, "Oh," and, "I wasn't aware of that." Perry pointed out helpfully that Brendan's brain was filled with hydrogen, like a blimp, and that it would float away if it weren't encased in his skull. Brendan got furious and called him a big bag of pigswill, and Uncle Hedge had to give them a look so that they'd simmer down, which Lala seemed to find amusing.

After pancakes we went out walking on the bluffs above the Sea Cove, which is nearly behind the house—behind Mrs. Hoover's house, really. The cliffs are high around the cove, and there's only a little bit of sand down on the horseshoe-shaped beach, which is mostly under water at high tide and is never very wide even when the tide is out, because the ocean bottom falls away so steeply there. Driftwood piles up on the rocks in the cove, and there's usually an immense lot of it, which you can use to build a fort, although if the tide comes up high enough, your fort floats away. After a storm you can find seashells there and stuff that gets washed up, like old shoes, although always just one. Once we found a coconut that had drifted in from across the ocean. It turned out to be full of salt water that had leaked into it, which we discovered after we hammered a hole in the top with a nail and paid Brendan a quarter to drink from it. Brendan didn't think it was as funny as Perry and I did.

Halfway up the cliffs, there's a cave in the rocks. It's not deep, but if it's rainy you can get in out of the wind and stay warm and dry, especially with a driftwood fire. You have to have a pail of water standing by in order to put the fire out when you leave. We take turns going down after the water, because it's hard to carry it back up. Brendan helped Lala climb across the face of the cliff toward the narrow little path to the cave. Unless you're Hasbro you have to hold on to scrubby bushes and roots that grow from the side of the cliff, and if you're not careful you might fall, which Brendan did once and broke his arm, as Ms Peckworthy already revealed. Hasbro just kind of dances across, because he's nimble despite his portliness. Perry says that dogs don't know anything about falling, and that's what makes them safe from it, although I don't know if that's scientific.

We started a fire with some of the dry wood that we had stowed there, and it was really jolly sitting and looking out at the ocean, which had calmed down since yesterday's storm. You might think you would suffocate having a fire in a cave, but the sea wind draws the smoke up the curve of the cave roof and out into the open air, so that you don't. If it's a calm day, though, really dead calm and not windy, there's no point in even trying to have a fire, because it would mean suffocation, which we found out the hard way one time.

In the summer you can spot whales from up there. You have to watch for their spray but sometimes there's dozens that go by in an afternoon, and you can see their dark shapes rising up out of the ocean and then disappearing again. There are otters, too, that come into the cove, and sea lions, and one time a sea elephant that was perfectly immense. It's the kind of place where you can sit for hours, listening to the sound of the waves crashing and the crying of the seagulls and the wind blowing across the cliffs with a kind of shuddery sound.

After a time we quit staring at the ocean and started talking, although none of us were asking what we were thinking: whether Lala had been at Lighthouse Beach yesterday morning and had peered in at the kitchen window last night. Maybe we didn't want to hear her lie about it. Lala took her atomizer out of the little bag she carried and spritzed herself on the face and arms. "It keeps my skin moist," she said, seeing that we were wondering about it.

"You've got very moist skin," Brendan said, gazing at her, or maybe at her skin.

Lala smiled at him, and said that she wanted to know more about our adventure with the Creeper, or at least Brendan's part in it. Then we asked her questions about Peach Manor, which was her home on Lake Windermere. I think she wanted to talk more than she wanted to listen, because once she got started she didn't stop, and that was fine, because all of it was strange and wonderful.

"What about old Cardigan Peach?" Perry asked her, Cardigan Peach being her grandfather. "We heard that he was *really* old. Over a hundred. Uncle Hedge says he was born before the automobile."

"Before *which* automobile?" Brendan asked. "There wasn't just one, you know."

"That's just a saying," Perry told him.

"Like 'old as Methuselah,'" I said.

"Or old as hydrogen," Perry said.

"He *is* old," Lala put in, before Brendan got himself into a state. She took a billfold out of her bag and showed us a picture of a man who looked a little bit like a human toad, his face being amphibious and goggle-eyed. I don't mean to be disrespectful, but that's what he *did* look like. He was dressed in a black cape and a little bow tie, and he carried a walking stick. He was standing by a pool of water enclosed by a stone ring, and he was looking down into the water, as if he saw something interesting in the depths. Lala told us about how her father, Giles Peach, was an inventor who had a workshop on the grounds of Peach Manor. Sometimes she didn't see him for days when he was inventing. He had built an anti-gravity vessel, she said, out of barrel hoops, an electric fan, and a wooden rowboat, with oars that rowed by themselves using a perpetual motion engine. It had floated up into space one night carrying a cargo of his smaller inventions and was by now out rowing among the stars.

Then she told us about the land at the Earth's core, where there were still dinosaurs because they had been protected from the great extinctions, and where there were cave people and mer-people, and where nature was still wild and unspoiled because there weren't any machines or factories or engines. She told us how you could sail into the hollow Earth aboard a hot air balloon by going farther and farther south until the oceans spilled over the edge of a vast hole into the interior seas. Without even knowing it you drifted downward, soon finding yourself inside the Earth instead of outside it, and when the balloon landed you were held to the walls by the centrifugal force of the spinning of the planet. It was just like gravity.

While Lala talked, rain clouds came in off the ocean, moving very quickly. Waves began to break against the shore one after another, so that the sound of the ocean was in our ears along with the crackling of the fire and the cries of seagulls. It soon began to rain, and the falling rain was like a curtain in front of us, so that we were completely sheltered from the world. There was the smell of new rain in the air, like when rain falls on a dry sidewalk, and there was a strange droning sound, as if hive of bees lived at the back of the cave. Lala's voice went on and on, very soft and even. It occurred to me that she was wandering somewhere in her own mind, lost in a memory, and was talking to herself.

And then the strangest thing happened. The rain stopped, the clouds evaporated like steam, and the sky grew clear and sunny. Out over the ocean there appeared an airship that was like an illustration in an old book. It was far away, and yet I could see it quite clearly. It was built of bundles of sticks or bamboo, and had a big whirling propeller that must have been making the beehive sound. The wings were like bat wings, and the tail was more like the tail of a fish than of an airplane. It was humming through the air, moving slowly. Beyond it, hazy and distant, there appeared immensely high dark cliffs, as if an island had risen out of the sea, and the airship was flying above the tall trees of that island, and in the sky around it flew prehistoric birds, turning and gliding. *Am I dreaming?* I wondered. But I wasn't.

After a time, I don't know how long, a gust of wind blew into the cave and billowed the smoke from the driftwood fire out through the cave mouth, hiding the world outside. When it cleared away again, the airship was gone and the prehistoric island along with it. The rainy, north coast day was as it had been. Brendan and Perry both had a look of astonishment on their faces, just like I must have had, but before anyone said anything about the impossible airship and island, we saw that Lala was pointing out to sea, at a fishing boat that was maybe a quarter mile offshore, turning in toward the cove and coming along straight toward us. Because of the deep water, you can actually bring a boat right in close, and for a moment that looked like what was happening, that he was going to run it right up onto the beach. But then the boat slowed and stopped some distance out, and we could see the man at the wheel. He put a spyglass to his eye and peered straight at us.

"It's *Wheyface the stinking Creeper*!" Perry said, for it was indeed him.

Lala ducked behind Brendan, who told her that she shouldn't be afraid, and that we had settled the Creeper's hash once and would do it again if he showed his ugly face. But of course he *was* showing his ugly face. We hadn't settled his hash or anything of the sort.

"Let's go," Perry said, "like Uncle Hedge told us."

I didn't have to be asked twice. The fire had burned down, but I made sure that the embers were out with seawater from the bucket, and then we made our way across the trail and up to the top of the bluffs. The boat was still down there, rising and falling on the swell. Brendan shook his fist and shouted bold things, and Lala told him he was very brave, and then she grabbed his hand and they took off running up the sea path like two lovebirds, and within moments we couldn't see them. When we looked back out to sea, the Creeper was turning the boat around and heading away.

Chapter 8

Ms Peckworthy
and the Smithfield

"It was Lala doing it," Perry said to me, as we came through the gate into the backyard. "Had to be—the island, the airship, the whole thing."

"Did you notice the humming noise?" I asked. "I thought it was a swarm of bees at first."

"So did I, but I think it was her. Not that *she* was humming. I don't mean that, but she was making it happen. It stopped when she was distracted by the Creeper's boat. Like it woke her up or something."

"Yes," Perry said. "That's it exactly. What we saw was mind projection, mass hallucination—the same things that she was seeing in her head."

The antenna was run up through the roof of the radio shed, which meant that Uncle Hedge was in there talking on his ham radio, which he calls "the Smithfield." I don't know why. The radio shed is built out of old lumber that Uncle Hedge and Mr. Vegeley got out of a barn that was being torn apart down in Little River. It's got many windows that they bought at yard sales and such, and some old painted metal signs nailed to it. One sign says "Penguin Ice, Fort Bragg," and there's another one that's a Humpty Dumpty with a crown on his head.

The radio looks nothing like a ham, really. It's very large, and most of the inside of the shed is taken up by the apparatus, which has about a thousand dials and lights and glass tubes that glow green and remind you of a deep tidepool on a sunny day. The whole thing makes bleeping and whistling sounds when the radio is warming up.

We went straight inside, where Uncle Hedge was listening hard to the radio speaker, and of course we waited for whoever it was to finish talking even though we were in a sweat to tell him about the appearance of the Creeper. "The fate of the Sleeper hangs in the balance..." the radio voice was saying, but then it suddenly fell silent. There was a burst of static followed by the sound of rickety old music for a moment before there was silence again. "For Pete's sake!" Uncle Hedge said, twisting a dial. It seemed like a good point to interrupt.

"The Creeper was in a boat in the Sea Cove just now," Perry told him.

"He turned around like he was going back out again," I said.

"North or south?" Uncle Hedge asked, getting up out of his chair.

"We don't know," I said. "We didn't wait to see."

"Just as well," he said. "Where's Lala?"

"In the house with Brendan," Perry told him.

And right then a figure appeared outside the window, trying to peer in, and I nearly jumped out of my wits. But it wasn't the Creeper; it was Ms Peckworthy, which was just as bad.

Uncle Hedge went to the door and looked out, saying, "So you've come to beard us in our den, Ms Peckworthy?"

"Well," she said, all flustery. "I didn't intend..." But peeping in at the window is one of the impolitest things there is, and if you peep you obviously intend to do it, so she was tongue tied, and besides that she was cramming something into her handbag—her notebook and pen. Uncle Hedge invited her to step in, and her eyes bugged out when she saw the radio, because who would have an enormous radio like that if he wasn't up to immense secret schemes? The radio speaker chose that moment to start up again, and the same weird voice said, "The Sleeper grows restless on his bed beneath the Earth," and then again it fell silent. Ms Peckworthy stood there blinking, as if the voice had made her forget where she was, and maybe even *who* she was.

She recollected herself and asked Uncle Hedge, "Who *was* that odd creature?"

"Which odd creature would that be?" Uncle Hedge asked politely.

"The tiny blond girl. She very nearly knocked me down going through the back gate just now. She dropped her carpetbag, and when I picked it up she didn't bother to thank me, but snatched it away and bolted down the path. I find that sort of behavior insufferable. Is she another one of yours?"

"We have her on loan," Uncle Hedge said. And then he looked at Perry and me and nodded toward the house, and I could see that he was worried about Lala even though he was still smiling. We ducked past Ms Peckworthy and ran in through the kitchen door, nearly tripping over Hasbro, who turned around and ran on ahead of us, as if he'd been coming to find us and now here we were. We followed him through the kitchen, and the first thing that we saw was that the Mermaid's box was open and the hand was sticking out—empty, with the fingers curled shut. Someone had taken the key.

We shouted Brendan's name but there was no answer. Hasbro started up the stairs and we followed him, still calling for Brendan, and when we went into Perry and Brendan's room we saw that the closet door was shut and that a wooden chair with a sweater laid across the top was shoved under the knob, as if the sweater was meant to muffle the sound of the chair knocking against the door. Hasbro put his nose to the door and barked, and we heard a voice from inside telling him to go away. It was Brendan, trapped.

But when we took the chair away and opened the door, he got mad at us. He didn't know he was trapped.

"Who locked you in?" I asked him.

"No one *locked* me in," he said. "Lala and I are playing hide and seek, and I'm hiding in the closet. Now if you'll kindly leave before you spoil everything..."

"Lala's gone off," Perry said. "Ms Peckworthy saw her on the sea path. She took her suitcase."

"Peckworthy's a scum-pig liar," Brendan said, getting really furious. (He can say *awful* things when he's angry, usually involving pigs, scum, swill, and filth, which he rearranges. When he's angry with himself it's worse.) "Lala's downstairs looking for me," he said, but I could see doubt in his eyes now.

"Who put the chair under the door knob?" I asked him.

"What door knob?"

"*This* door knob!" Perry shouted. "Lala sneaked in and slipped it under there! What we want to know is did *you* take the Mermaid's key?"

For a moment he looked surprised and frightened both, and I didn't blame him. "No," he said in a small voice. "You're always accusing me."

"*Someone's* opened the box," I said, "and the key's not there. Nobody's accusing you. It was Lala who took it."

"She played on your affections like Nero played the fiddle," Perry said, "and Rome burned in the offing."

"Stow it, can't you?" Brendan said, but the truth was obvious, even to him. Lala had taken the key and gone, and she had taken her stuff with her because she wasn't coming back. She had hoaxed us. We ran back out to the radio shed to report this to Uncle Hedge, just as Ms Peckworthy was leaving. She looked at Brendan as if she thought he was some kind of culprit, but then she saw the terrible Hasbro coming along behind us and she put her back to the wall, just in case she had to fight him off.

"That animal is a menace," she said.

"He's a pure bred peccadillo," Uncle Hedge told her, "half peccary and half armadillo," and then he looked significantly at me, and I shook my head to signify that Lala was gone.

"Well, I know nothing about dogs," Ms Peckworthy said. "You mark my words, then, Mr. Hedgepeth—I'm keeping an eye on these children."

"An eyeball peeled for the great big shoe, eh? I'm in your debt, Ms Peckworthy, although I'm monstrously busy right now. Allow me to show you to the gate. We're just going in that direction ourselves."

"A big shoe? No doubt that's meant to be humorous. And, by the way, there's a particularly shady looking man lurking below the bluffs. I saw him motoring ashore in a small boat—a perfectly awful, treacherous looking character. If these three children were mine, I'd keep them in the house with the doors locked, Mr. Hedgepeth. You mark my words...."

But we never learned what words to mark, because all of us, Uncle Hedge included, were running out toward the sea path now and down along the bluffs, and Ms Peckworthy was left talking to the air. We saw the Creeper halfway to the bottom of the trail down the cliff, carrying Lala over his shoulder like a sack of grain, holding onto her with one hand as he half-climbed and half-slid down the steep path, kicking rocks loose with the heels of his boots. Her tapestry bag lay on the beach far below, where the Creeper had no doubt thrown it.

Brendan shouted and scrambled rashly down after him, and the Creeper looked back up at us, lost his footing, and for a moment stood there just barely balanced, waving his free arm like a windmill. I thought he would fall for sure, and Lala with him, but instead he sat down hard and started sliding, still holding onto her, sliding faster and faster until he sort of threw himself to the side and made a wild grab at a heavy root alongside the path.

Uncle Hedge yelled at Brendan to stop, but Brendan shouted, "I can catch him!" and kept going. Perry followed him down and so did I, because I could see that Brendan wasn't going to stop, no matter what, and it would have been bad for him to battle the Creeper by himself if he *did* catch him. Uncle Hedge started down behind us, shouting warnings at us, and when I looked back up at him, I saw Ms Peckworthy above on the sea path, with her mouth gaping open and her eyes wide with astonishment. If she wanted proof that we were "up to something" she had enough now to fill her notebook.

The Creeper lurched to his feet, still carrying Lala, and he loped down the last twenty feet of trail and straight out onto the sand and rocks where there was a little motorboat moored. Lala was pounding him on the back with her fists and yelling, but he simply ignored her as he dumped her into the boat, picked up her tapestry bag and dumped that in too, and then shoved off, yanking twice on the rope to start the engine, and steering straight out to sea. The fishing boat that we had seen earlier was floating on the swell some distance out. They didn't have far to go.

Brendan leaped down onto the beach now and stood at the water's edge. But like I said before, it quickly gets deep, and Brendan can't swim well, so that was the end of the chase. If they had been closer to shore, I think Brendan would have jumped in, because he can be rash when he's riled up, and of course he was desperately in love with Lala even though she had fiddled with his trust. He threw some rocks, which wasn't a well thought out idea, because one of them thunked into the boat and nearly hit Lala. She turned and looked back at us and then stood up, and I believe that she was going to leap overboard, but the Creeper lunged forward and grabbed a handful of her dress and sat her back down. The boat went all swervy in the water so that a wave hit it sideways and nearly capsized it. But in a moment they were headed out to sea again, and there wasn't a single thing that we could do about it but go back up, which we did.

By the time we were at the top again the Creeper and Lala were already aboard the fishing boat and the Creeper was getting away clean. The five of us took off running again, right past Ms Peckworthy. We didn't stop to chat, but ran all the way home to the Zeuglodon and piled in. When we headed down the driveway I looked back, and there was Ms Peckworthy, coming along in a hurry and gaping at us. She didn't get much of a gape, because we zoomed away, straight down to the Coast Highway where we turned north toward Fort Bragg, which is the closest harbor to Caspar and was perhaps the Creeper's destination.

I won't reveal how abashed Brendan was when he told Uncle Hedge about showing Lala how to open the Mermaid's box—only because she had asked him so nicely—and then how she had suggested they play hide and seek. I started feeling bad for Brendan, because *he* didn't steal the key; he had only showed Lala how to open the box, and he had done that because she had played upon his affections, as Perry had put it. She had hoaxed us all, even Uncle Hedge. And what about me? I hadn't trusted her from the start, but there was no joy in being right about her, because all it meant was that I was a bigger fool than anyone for not speaking up. So we were all as glum as hedgehogs, even Hasbro.

After we had all taken turns blaming ourselves, Uncle Hedge pointed out that besides being a slippery character, Lala was also the granddaughter of Basil Peach, and so she had to be found and recovered from the Creeper, whatever it took.

We turned off onto a viewpoint over the ocean, but there was no fishing boat to be seen, which meant that perhaps the Creeper was hugging the shore and so was hidden by the cliffs. It also might mean that he had doubled back and gone away south rather than north. We drove down to the harbor, but he wasn't there either. It soon became evident that he wasn't anywhere, and that we were burning daylight and couldn't just sit around waiting for him to turn up, so we drove over to police headquarters and talked to Captain Smith again, who called the Coast Guard straightaway and put them on the lookout for the fishing boat and the Creeper.

It took two days for them to find it, run aground on a lonesome beach ten miles down the coast. The Creeper's car was abandoned at the Little River Airport with the keys still in the ignition. Captain Smith identified it with the photos he had taken of the tire tread out on the bluffs.

Lala had come all the way out to Caspar from Lake Windermere to fetch the Mermaid's key, because she was worried that the Creeper would find it first. Now she had played right into his hands just by fate, and the Creeper would have the key after all, and she was a prisoner.

Chapter 9

The Incident
of the Notebook

A couple of days after the kidnapping we were eating cold spaghetti and meat sauce sandwiches for breakfast, sitting at the kitchen table. Uncle Hedge had taken his sandwich out to the radio shed where he was trying to get through to other members of the Guild of St. George, especially Basil Peach, who can be difficult to find if he can be found at all. Uncle Hedge was in a dither to find him, but it would turn out that somebody else would find Uncle Hedge first.

Brendan spread extra butter on the outside of his bread, leaving room along the edge so that his fingers wouldn't get smeary. "What I'm wondering about," he said between bites, "is Peckworthy." He gestured with his fork and squinted up his eyes like he does when he wants you to think he has secret knowledge.

"Half a penny for your thoughts," Perry said to him. "The other half we'll give to the elves. Perkins, fetch a penny and the kitchen shears."

"I mean, what's Peckworthy's *real* game?" Brendan said, ignoring him.

"We know what her game is," I said. "We heard her say what it was. Now it's the end of the week, and she's still here with her notebook. That's what I'm worried about. What if today's the day that she comes for us?"

"*If* that's her game," Brendan observed.

"What else is she doing with her notebook," Perry asked, "drawing pictures of birds?"

"Okay, then tell me who she was waiting for at the Skunk Train that night when the Creeper broke into the museum."

"*Us.* She followed us," I told him. "We've seen her car other times. She's not trying to hide."

"What if she wasn't following anyone?" Brendan said. "What if she was *waiting* for someone?"

I started making another sandwich, because I'm always hungry around cold spaghetti sandwiches. You put a lot of butter on the bread and an inch of yesterday's spaghetti, right out of the fridge. It's good hot, too, but the spaghetti gets slippery with the butter and slides out of the sandwich, so cold works better, although it's goopy. "You're saying that she's in league with the Creeper?" I asked.

Brendan nodded very slowly and ponderously. "*The getaway car,*" he said. "There's *always* a getaway car."

"The Creeper can't drive himself around?" Perry asked. "Why would he need Frau Peckworthy to drive him? She didn't drive him down to the bluffs that day he tried to snatch you. He had his own car, remember?"

"Of course," Brendan said. "But how did the Creeper know that's where we were going? I'll tell you why. Peckworthy called him and told him we were on the way. That's what she was doing in the neighborhood. She was a scout for the Creeper."

"Creeper, the game's afoot!" Perry said in a Peckworthy-like voice. "Sounds like arrant madness. Methinks you've lent your sanity to the apes."

"We've *got* to find out what's in the notebook," Brendan said. "We'll lay in wait for her. We have to."

"I think you mean *lie* in wait," Perry told him.

"I know what I mean," Brendan said. "Don't always be telling me what I mean."

"Uncle Hedge told us not to give Ms Peckworthy any more things to write about," I said, "so no one's going to do any lying in wait."

Brendan shrugged and smiled, but before we could argue, the kitchen door opened and Uncle Hedge walked in, looking like a man in a hurry. "Pack your bags," he said. "We haven't a moment to lose."

The message had come in over the Smithfield on the sublunar frequency, which sometimes picks up radio talk from ships at sea. You can hear them yammering away in Russian or Australian or some other language. That's just what had happened. Uncle Hedge got a call from a ship nearly four thousand miles away, although it wasn't a Russian or an Australian. It was Dr. Hilario Frosticos himself, aboard his submarine, calling with a ransom demand.

He wanted the missing pages from the Peach notebook, he said. And he wanted the Mermaid's key. He would trade them for Lala, straight across. He had no use for the little girl, only for the maps and the key, but he was getting impatient. "This time you'll come to *me*, Hedgepeth," he said, and then told him that he would make the swap far out in the North Atlantic, where there would be no clever tricks. At the sign of clever tricks he would disappear like a ghost and Lala would find herself in deep water. "Literally," he said, and that was the end of the message.

Of course we didn't have the key. Lala had the key, but that made no difference at all. It wasn't something that Uncle Hedge would reveal to Frosticos. That would have to come out in the wash, Uncle Hedge told us.

That morning was a holiday for students, what's called an "in-service" day—the only day of the year when teachers have school and students don't. We went to school anyway, except not to go to class, but to talk to our teachers and to the Principal, Mr. Diggler. Next week was spring break, you see, but we couldn't be sure just when we'd return from our voyage. (Of course we couldn't say why we were going.) Mr. Collier, my science teacher, said that I should put together a photographic diary of interesting scientific things that I saw during our sea voyage, and for my English class I had to write about it, which is part of what you're reading now. Perry had to work on his lexicon of significant words. Brendan had a two-page list of assignments that was mostly make-up for things he hadn't finished but should have, so he was dismal as we walked down to Mr. Diggler's office to get his approval.

We opened the door to Student Services, and who should we see walking out of the Principal's office but Ms Henrietta Peckworthy herself, looking considerably pickled. She gave us a decisive look, like she had our number, and nodded slowly at us before passing on. It was the second worst moment in my life. Everything changed in the instant I saw her, like in movies where someone looks up and Death is standing there wearing a black robe and hood, reaching out to touch you.

Mr. Diggler came out of his office then, and Uncle Hedge shook his hand. Mr. Diggler asked after Mr. Vegeley, and Uncle Hedge said that Mr. Vegeley was as hearty as an alligator, and Mr. Diggler said that he was happy to hear it. Mr. Diggler is a short man, thin and nervous and slow and newt-like. Sometimes unworthy students frighten him very badly by sneaking up behind him and exploding inflated lunch sacks, which causes him to leap into the air and shout.

I've never done this, although other people I won't mention have done it and have always managed to run away before Mr. Diggler recovered his wits and turned around to catch the culprit.

"If my eyes don't deceive me," Uncle Hedge said to Mr. Diggler, "that was Ms Henrietta Peckworthy."

"Yes, it was," Mr. Diggler agreed. "She's a tenacious woman. Very tenacious. She won't be put off. This is her third visit to the school."

"She gets her fair share of worms," Uncle Hedge said.

"Worms?" Mr. Diggler asked, blinking his eyes slowly, which brought out his newt-likeness.

"He means she's the early bird," Perry said helpfully.

"That's the truth," Mr. Diggler said. "I'm afraid she means trouble, too." He glanced at us, as if he was worried about us overhearing.

"You can speak plainly," Uncle Hedge told him. "Ms Peckworthy isn't anyone's secret."

"She had drawn up...papers of some sort," Mr. Diggler said, "which only had to be certified somehow by social services, and..." He noticed then that there was a woman's handbag lying on a chair. The office window looked out onto the parking lot, and we could see Ms Peckworthy still sitting in her car. Then the car door swung open, and she climbed out again.

"Someone run it on out to her," Uncle Hedge said.

Perry started to pick up the handbag, but Brendan said, "I'll do it," and he pushed Perry aside, snatched up the bag, and went out through the door running. After a moment—a long moment—we saw him crossing the parking lot. Ms Peckworthy poked her head forward like a surprised pigeon when she saw him rushing at her, but then she must have seen her handbag, because she stepped forward and took it from Brendan, and the excitement was over.

When Brendan came back in there was something in his face that made me wonder, although it wasn't until later, when we got home and were getting ready to go to the airport, that he pulled Ms Peckworthy's notebook out from under his sweater. He looked triumphant. He hadn't had to lie in wait for her at all, but had taken the notebook right out of her handbag before he got to the parking lot. I reminded him that we had voted against stealing the notebook, and that I had been against it from the start, and that stealing it was wrong.

"Dry up, Perkins," Brendan told me unpleasantly. "If you don't like it, don't look at it." He decided not to let Perry look at it either. He said he was going down to the sea cave that very moment to look at it himself, and to burn it. A half hour later, when he returned, he wouldn't tell Perry or me what actually *was* in the notebook, but said he would die with the secret safe in his head, even if he was tortured, and so I said the sooner the better, although later I felt bad about saying it. I also felt bad, in a small way, that I very much wanted to know what was in the notebook, and also that part of me was *glad* that Brendan had stolen it and burned it.

As you can imagine, we were in a sweat to leave for the airport because of what Mr. Diggler had said about the papers. Time was passing like a tortoise or a sloth, both of which are slow, and so we spent it up in the attic, watching through the gable window for Ms Peckworthy's car to turn up into the neighborhood. The notebook might be a heap of ashes now, but we still weren't easy about it, because Perry pointed out that the notebook wasn't really evidence of anything, but only a record of the evidence. Brendan said that she would never take him alive, and that he had an escape route down the bluffs to his "hideout," by which he meant the lighthouse. He thought that the unlocked window was a secret that only he knew about. Our suitcases already lay in the trunk of the Zeuglodon along with the Mermaid in her box, and I was itching to be in the back seat watching the scenery fly past.

Uncle Hedge came home at last, laden with supplies for the long flight ahead, and so we hurried back down to the livingroom. He carried the missing maps from the Peach journals along with the rest. They were bound up in a lead box that he had dipped in wax in case they had to be thrown overboard to sink into the ocean if we were betrayed. Uncle Hedge had cleverly hidden a radio locater inside the box so that they could be found again. We locked up the house and set out, Hasbro included, and drove on down to the airport at Little River, carrying doughnuts and cocoa in a thermos and a basket lunch, because you really can't eat airplane food and be happy about it. There was no sign of Ms Peckworthy, and that was the best part of all, but I knew that I wouldn't stop being nervous about her until we were in the air. One thing we found out at the airport was that Lala Peach had booked a flight into San Francisco the very morning that she stole the key and ran for it, although of course she never got a chance to use the ticket. From San Francisco she was booked into Manchester, England. She hadn't come out to "visit" at all. Just like the Creeper, she had come out merely to steal the key. She had been better than the Creeper at stealing it, although not so good at getting away.

It was a beautiful sunny day, with just a few floating clouds, and the salty ocean wind smelling like freedom when we walked out onto the tarmac toward the plane. The Creeper's car was gone, and the parking lot of the airport was nearly deserted except for the Zeuglodon, which Mr. Vegeley would pick up later in the day, and then drive it home and lock it in the garage. In no time at all we found ourselves taxiing down the runway, picking up speed, and finally angling up into the air, the buildings below dwindling in size.

I had just settled back in my seat when Perry said, "There she comes! The worthy Ms Peck!" He was pointing out the window toward the ground, so we crowded around to look. Sure enough, Ms Peckworthy's red car, looking like a toy car now, was just then pulling into the airport parking lot. For one bad moment I thought that she would still be able to stop us—that the pilot would put on the brakes, or whatever you put on when you're flying, and we would fall into her clutches after all. But that didn't happen. Ms Peckworthy got out of her car, tiny as a bug, and stood there looking up at us as until we disappeared into a cloud. When we came out into blue sky again, she was lost behind us, and there was nothing but the tree-covered mountains of the Coast Range below and the shimmering ocean away on the right.

Chapter 10

Aboard the *S. S. Clematis*

ff the southeast coast of Newfoundland there's a cold ocean current called the Labrador Current, which flows down out of the Labrador Sea and the frozen arctic waters in the north. A warm current called the Gulf Stream comes up from the south and heats the air above it, and when this warm air over the Gulf Stream meets the cold air above of the Labrador Current, it generates fog like a great huge machine. For days and weeks the fog doesn't clear up, because there's always more fog being made, and it's so thick that when you're standing on deck you can't be sure whether you're looking out at gray ocean water or at a curtain of fog.

Old Captain Sodbury taught us about currents on board ship. It's the kind of thing they can tell you in a science class, but what they can't tell you is what it's like to *be* there, in the midst of it. There are clear places in the fog, like hidden rooms, and suddenly the ship would sail out into one of those clear spaces with the sun shining and glittering on the water, and it's so bright that you have to squint your eyes. Behind you and way off in front of you and to either side are the gray walls, swirling and moving as if they're full of restless ghosts, but you're no longer part of the fog or of those ghosts, but are alone on your own little patch of sunlit ocean. The sound of the ship's engines and the calling of the sea birds that fish over the Grand Banks are suddenly clear and sharp instead of muffled by wet air, and the world is as strange as waking up from a dream. Then you slip back through the misty curtain, and the sunlight disappears behind you, and the world is gray again.

The Grand Banks are of course not the sort of banks where you put your money, but are a shallow, rocky shelf that rises near the surface of the ocean. They stretch almost three hundred miles off Newfoundland into the Atlantic. Sometimes in the winter entire icebergs float down out of the Arctic Sea and run aground on the Banks and get stuck and just sit there melting and melting. It's a part of the ocean known for strange things occurring, and you can be sure that I kept my camera in my pocket.

During the 1870s giant squids fifty feet long and with suckers as big around as car tires came up out of deep water by the dozen and washed ashore in Newfoundland, although no one knows why, and then after a time they stopped washing ashore, and nothing like that has ever happened again, at least not with giant squids. That was called "the Newfoundland groundings." Maybe some day there will be giant squids off Caspar, although I hope they don't ground themselves, because a live squid is so very much better than a dead one, which is true of almost everything.

So that's where we found ourselves, on board the S.S. Clematis, sailing out of St. John's, Newfoundland, under Captain William Sodbury, whom Uncle Hedge sailed with in the old days, when they were young. The ship is an old Merchant Marine vessel, but small—only about thirty meters, which didn't seem all that small to me. According to Uncle Hedge it was "overhauled" and has powerful magnet-drive Helmoltz engines based on a design by Roycroft

Squires, who was an engineer in Los Angeles back in the 1950s. The Guild of St. George bought his patents and rebuilt the *Clematis*, which looks like an old Merchant Marine vessel on the outside, and sounds like one, too, but that's really just a disguise, what Uncle Hedge calls "window dressing." I wanted to take photographs of the engines and other interesting things for my science project, but they were top secret, and so I couldn't.

The *Clematis* has three decks: the boat deck, the cabin deck or 'tween deck, and what's called the below-deck. We were on the cabin deck, which has thirteen staterooms for passengers on account of there being thirteen members of the Guild of St. George, so we each had one of our own. They were small and snug, with porthole windows and just enough cupboard space to stow your gear. There's a saloon on the cabin deck, too, and the galley and the library and the chart room, which is hung with maps of the coasts and seas of the world, and with hundreds more charts and maps in wooden drawers. The *Clematis* travels all over the watery deep, you see, on scientific expeditions and doing the bidding of the Guild.

Perry and I had very little to do on the voyage, being mostly caught up with our work at school. I took pictures of the fog, and pictures of not-fog, but they weren't interesting. There were books in the library, though, and I spent hours reading by the misty light coming in through the porthole. Lots of times I would stop reading and just look at things and get lost in my own thoughts. The walls were paneled with dark wood, and there were brass fittings and fixtures and Turkish carpets of rich colors. There were paintings of sailing ships on the walls, tossing on the high seas, and a portrait of Admiral Nelson and another one of Sir Francis Drake. The Mermaid sat on the wooden library table, which was carved around the edges with the figures of South Seas fishes, and sometimes I had the strangest feeling that she was about to speak to me, to tell me secret things about the world beneath our ship. She kept silent, though.

When we were off the Grand Banks themselves, the sound of fog horns was frequent, and there was the ringing of ships' bells, and the *Clematis* moved slowly in order not to collide with anything, either ships or out-of-the-way icebergs, which I wanted very much to see in order to take photos of something solid. But there was still too much fog, really, to see anything. How we were going to find a submarine that was the color of the fog itself was a question worth pondering, but Uncle Hedge said that we didn't have to find it, really. We were waiting to be contacted on the shipboard sub-lunar. Dr. Frosticos would give us coordinates and instructions. In the meantime we were simply biding our time.

As a science project, Brendan undertook an experiment with fog. Uncle Hedge told him that he must follow the scientific method, with a hypothesis, and that he must prove or disprove the hypothesis in the end, because a paper without a conclusion isn't a paper at all. Brendan's hypothesis, which wasn't much of a one, was that fog vanished when you put it into a jar, and so fog wasn't really anything at all but was an illusion. He went and begged six jars with lids from the steward, old Charlie Slimmerman, who only eats half of anything on his plate, which is why he's slim. His real last name is Panguitch, but he doesn't use it because it reminds him of food. Brendan took the jars out to the bow of the ship and "caught" the fog in them and screwed on the tops, just like the jar with Edison's last breath in it, and sure enough, when he brought the bottles back inside they appeared to be empty.

He wrote his paper in about ten minutes and said his hypothesis was proved, and that fog was imaginary. Uncle Hedge said that his paper was a travesty and must be at least four pages long and have a sensible method in order to have a sensible result. So Perry and I kindly said we would help him do the experiment over again. We took the jars back out onto the deck, and we all worked to fill them with the bellows from the library fireplace, sucking up fog with the bellows and then shooting it into the jars through a hole in a piece of plastic wrap stretched over the top. We screwed the lids down as soon as we pulled the bellows out of the jars, but somehow all the fog escaped no matter how quick we were, and the jars remained empty.

"I've got it!" Brendan said finally. "Fog *isn't* imaginary, but just moves really *fast*, like light. How fast does light go?"

"Two point six zillion miles an hour," Perry told him. "In one light year it can reach the solar plexus, maybe farther."

"Then my hypothesis is that fog moves at the speed of two point six zillion miles an hour," Brendan said, "and that it won't stand to be in a jar. It's like a genie in a lamp. It escapes at the first chance, so fast that you can't even see. You measure it in fog years."

"Is that like dog years?" Perry asked.

"Much faster," Brendan said haughtily.

"There's your title," Perry said helpfully, "'Faster than a dog year.'"

"There's your *brain*, you mean," Brendan said.

"And your hypothesis is stupid as a stick."

"Did *you* see the fog inside the jar?" Brendan asked him.

"No. But I didn't see a dinosaur inside the jar either. Was there one of those, too, but it jumped out really fast?"

"Talk about stupid as a stick," Brendan said. "Who said anything about dinosaurs?"

"He means you can't just keep changing your hypothesis when the experiment doesn't work," I told him sensibly. "That's backwards science."

"Who made *you* the queen of the world?" Brendan asked nastily. "Talk about backwards. And anyway, my way is more righter than yours, because whatever happens *becomes* the hypothesis. That's how Newton invented gravity. The apple hit him in the head, and that's when he knew about it. And the same with what's-his-name—that man in the bathtub who sloshed out all the water on the floor and then figured out it was because he was too fat."

"Archimedes," I said. "And he wasn't a fat man."

"How do *you* know? Were you there? I think he was a fat man, and I think that he should have put less water in the bathtub. *I* could have told him that much, the scum-pig moron."

"Archimedes wasn't a moron," I said calmly. "And Newton didn't *invent* gravity. And the apple didn't hit him in the head anyway."

But Brendan wouldn't listen. He said that *he* was the scientist, in case we'd forgotten, and that we were just Igor, and we were as ugly as Igor, too, and as stupid as Archimedes. Perry said that Brendan could jolly well *be* the scientist, then, because he was going off to the library to read a book, and that he could hardly wait to hear what Uncle Hedge would have to say about Brendan's brilliant hypothesis.

Brendan told me that I was "dismissed," and so I left, too. I walked toward the bow, feeling lazy and bored and just looking out at the fog and thinking about Newton and gravity and whether it would be funny if it had been a fig instead of an apple, which made me realize I was hungry. So I decided to look in on the galley to beg an apple from Wise Norton, the ship's pegleg cook, who would be putting together lunch. I heard voices ahead just then, but the fog was so thick that I didn't see anyone, although they must be close by. I could smell pipe smoke, too, so it was Captain Sodbury, or at least one of them was.

I stopped, not really meaning to eavesdrop, but not moving along, either, and once the talking got going again, I stayed to listen.

"I never gave this talk about the Sleeper much credence," the Captain said. "It sounds like nonsense to me. Tolerably unlikely."

"I've seen old Cardigan Peach at work"—it was Uncle Hedge now—"and I came to believe things that I wouldn't admit in public, if you know what I mean. There's no room for it in science, what I saw."

"I've seen such things myself," Captain Sodbury said. "In '62, when I was first apprenticed to the Guild, I was ship's boy on the old *Wisteria*, down along the coast of Brazil. We put out a boat one midnight to pick up a man on a beach right there at the mouth of the Amazon, on one of those islands off Marajo. The man was Basil Peach, although the name meant nothing to me at the time. I was keyed up, you know, because the Captain told us there was some danger from interlopers. It was dark, too, and unless the man had a light and could show us a glim, there wasn't much hope of us finding him. There's a hundred miles of shoreline there."

"But you found Peach?"

"Aye, we found him. It was me who saw him. There were clouds, you see, with the crescent moon showing through now and again, but mostly black as pitch, and you couldn't tell the beach from the ocean. Then out comes the moon, looking like the cat's smile, only it seems to me to be falling right down out of the sky, like it'll land in the ocean, and by and by I could see the clouds *behind* it. The tropical air can play some tricks on you, but this beat all.

"So everyone was looking at the sky, you see, with the moon dropping straight toward us like it was hung with lead weights. I took a squint at the shore, and the moonlight looked like half a ring of witchfire where it was reflected on the sand, although it was dark beyond. There stood Basil Peach in the midst of it, wearing that hat of his and glowing with moonlight. I sung out, and we headed in toward shore, and the moon hung there spanning half the sky until we run the boat up onto the sand and Peach was safe. Then away it went, back up into its rightful orbit, and the clouds covered it, and we pushed off and back to the ship in the darkness with no one saying much of anything but everyone thinking the same way. Like you said, there was nothing natural in it. I didn't know Peach from an apricot, but I when I saw the man up close there in the boat I knew he'd done it himself. He drew the moon out of the sky like a lantern when he had a need of it."

I thought about what we had seen at the sea cave, and I knew the Captain was right. Lala Peach could do it, too, or something like it.

"This Sleeper business is a different kettle of fish, though," Captain Sodbury said. "I can understand what they call 'mind projection.' But the idea that the rest of us can... *participate* in it—that's too many for me."

"And yet there's evidence of it," Uncle Hedge said.

"Stories, maybe. I haven't seen what you'd call evidence."

"Stories that convinced the Doctor, right enough. Otherwise he wouldn't be out here holding Lala Peach for ransom. What I want to know is what he intends to *do*. He's got his eye on getting through the Windermere Passage while Giles Peach is asleep and dreaming, but Peach will wake up, and then what?"

"That's beyond my ken," the Captain said. "The spring tide is five days away. There's always a spring tide in this business of the Sleeper, or so they say."

"That's why Frosticos is in such a tearing hurry," Uncle Hedge said. "It makes him a dangerous man. He knows something that we don't about all this, but what is it? What's his game?"

"Maybe he aims to get in through the Passage and back out again before Peach wakes up and closes it down. There's something Frosticos wants to bring out, I'd say."

"So I thought. But I'm starting to think there's more. Whatever he's aiming to do, it frightened Lala into coming out to Fort Bragg to get hold of the key. She was in the same kind of hurry. We know that now. If the Doctor was after a bucketful of diamonds, why would *she* care about what he did? It's no loss to her. To my mind she means to put a stop to something more sinister than anything you can carry in a bucket, and she means to do it alone. She doesn't trust anyone outside the family."

It was right then that the *Clematis* sailed out of the fog and into one of those clear spaces that I told you about, and my iceberg wish came true. Lying a quarter mile off the starboard bow was a floating ice island. The ice was blue along the edges, a deep aqua blue like the color of the Zeuglodon. I guess you could call it an iceberg, except that it had a long, low area along one edge, like a beach, and so it looked more like an island than like a berg. "There she blows," Captain Sodbury said, and Uncle Hedge said, "I guess it's time." They were standing ten feet from me, but the fog had been so thick a minute ago that we'd all been invisible.

I watched the nearby ocean for the appearance of a submarine, but there was no submarine to be seen. The ship's engines fell off, and we ghosted along for a moment and then stopped dead still. The anchors rattled down and quickly found the bottom, because as I said, it's shallow in those seas. I took pictures of the island and of the small waves breaking along the beach, and Uncle Hedge watched the island through binoculars. Hasbro prowled up and down, sniffing the cold air, as if he knew something was about to happen, and Brendan and Perry came on deck. Perry said, "Crikey," but Brendan said nothing at all.

Rising above the beach were steep ice cliffs, one behind the other, with a dark valley in between two of the highest. As we watched, an enormous long chunk of ice broke away along the farther edge of the island and fell crashing into the sea, sending up a plume of water and a wave that ran out away from the island and soon passed beneath us. I was anxious to go across and actually walk on the ice myself, which Uncle Hedge had said we might do if he thought it was safe.

"Look there!" Perry said suddenly, just as a man walked out from within the shadows of the ice valley. He was curiously dressed, but it wasn't until Uncle Hedge handed me the binoculars that I could make any sense out of his strange garb, and even then it was hard to believe. Over his head he wore a diver's helmet made out of what looked like an enormous spiral seashell, and the sunlight glanced off its circular glass faceplate. There were two hoses spiraling away over his shoulders, connected to a cylinder suspended in front of his stomach by a strap that went around his neck. He was dressed in a baggy pair of pantaloons with a long overcoat with a fur collar.

"It's Reginald Peach," Uncle Hedge said in a low voice. "Back from the dead. I'll be dipped in a sack of dung."

Chapter 11

The Ice Island

"Aye, it's Reginald," Captain Sodbury said. "It appears that he's gone over to the other side."

Uncle Hedge shook his head. "I don't think so," he said. "There's always been bad blood between him and Basil, but he wouldn't harm Lala. She's his grand niece after all. It's a mystery what he's doing here, but either we'll know the truth soon enough, or we'll be homeward bound and it won't matter."

Uncle Hedge turned around and went back into the ship, heading down the companionway in the direction of the chart room, and when he returned he was carrying the lead-encased box with the journal maps inside. As he walked he slipped them into a canvas bag on a strap and hung it around his neck. Like I said, if things went bad, and we were betrayed, the lead box was meant to carry the maps to the bottom of the sea. But if Frosticos kept his word, and handed over Lala, then Uncle Hedge was to give him the box, and just like that Frosticos would have won. What we would do then, or what Lala would do, I didn't know. There was the matter of the key, also, and I wondered whether they would have any idea by now that Lala possessed it. Uncle Hedge would have to tell them, of course, to keep up his side of the bargain, and then they'd have to take it away from Lala. What a mess, I thought.

Charlie Slimmerman handed us each a pair of strap-on ice cleats—attachable shoe soles with spikes sticking through for walking on ice. He told us not to put them on yet, because we didn't want to punch holes in the bottom of the boat, which was an inflatable. He also gave us a big tin box with a lunch inside, and then he and Captain Sodbury lowered the inflatable into the water and put down the ladder. The four of us were going across, while Charlie, the Captain, Wise Norton, and Hasbro stayed behind.

We climbed down into the inflatable and I started the outboard motor (which is one of things I'm good at, because my mother taught me) and all the time I was afraid that Uncle Hedge would change his mind and decide that it was too dangerous for us, but he didn't. We were to stay well back, he told us, and under no circumstances were we to come anywhere near the negotiations, which shouldn't take more than sixty seconds, because he intended to keep his word and hand over the maps. If anything "went south" as he put it, we were to head straight back to the ship in the inflatable, even if it meant leaving him behind.

I steered us toward the distant beach, very carefully and slowly, too, so that we didn't ship any water. A few yards off, I cut the power, and we cocked the engine forward so that the propeller wouldn't get damaged beating against the ice. The inflatable slid up onto the ice shelf, riding a small wave, and we climbed out, putting on our ice cleats and crunching up the beach toward the man in the seashell helmet.

Uncle Hedge said, "What ho, Reginald," and they shook hands, and Reginald said, "Come see, come saw," which I didn't at all understand. He said this in a bubbly way, because—and you're not going to believe this—the seashell helmet that encased his head was *full of water,* just the opposite of a diver's helmet. One of the two hoses ran the water through the canister at his waist, something called a "carbon dioxide scrubber," and the other hose ran the "scrubbed" air back into his helmet, so that he always had oxygenated water to breathe. Why he breathed water instead of air is a Peach family mystery, as are Lala's gills and webbed fingers and other things even stranger, things that we didn't know at the time but were going to find out. The helmet had a built-in voice box so that Reginald could talk, but as I said, he sounded bubbly.

"Haven't...gone over, have you?" Uncle Hedge asked him in a low voice, and Reginald shook his head. And then, taking great care, he held up a small piece of paper with the words, "He's listening," written on it. When Uncle Hedge had read it, Reginald put the paper into his coat pocket very casually. He made a little jerk of his head, then, toward the ice cliff behind him. When I looked I could see what appeared to be a round, white disk with holes in it, set flat in the ice right there in the face of the cliff, and I knew in an instant what it was—a listening device. We weren't on one of the random, floating icebergs that had strayed down from the Arctic; we were on an iceberg inhabited by Dr. Hilario Frosticos, and he could overhear our every word.

As soon as we knew that, we didn't utter very many words at all, but followed Reginald up the narrow valley between walls of ice that rose away on either side. Seen from up close, the ice wasn't so immensely blue, but it was quite clear. The valley floor was littered with ice chunks, and we had to step over the small ones and slip between the large ones. It was slow going, and although it seemed to me to be taking a long time, probably we hadn't gone more than a hundred yards before we went around a corner and there before us lay a lake of calm water.

It wasn't a real lake, but was the ocean itself, sheltered from the wind and waves by the barrier of ice around it. The floating ice island was actually a great ring of ice cliffs, and we had gotten to the center of it. The surface of the lake was as smooth as a sheet of glass, and the air was quiet and still, and not nearly so cold as it had been on the beach. I could see schools of fish beneath the calm water, and deeper yet there were slowly moving black shapes, perfectly enormous—sharks, maybe, or some variety of whale.

There in front of us lay the submarine, ghostly white and moored to a pier that was built right into the ice. There was a wooden shed at the top end of the pier with a stovepipe sticking out of the roof and some fishing poles in a rack against an outside wall. On beyond the pier lay two more shacks on the ice, each with its own stovepipe. There was firewood stacked nearby the shacks as well as some wooden casks of the sort that might hold salted meat or pickles. The shacks were built of scraps of driftwood and broken up pieces of ships, and they had porthole windows and roofs made up of odds and ends of things, including sheets of tin and old wooden doors.

The submarine itself looked something like a great fish—not like a modern submarine at all. It had a line of pointed fins at the back, angled toward its tail, and great glass windows in front like eyes, and around those windows and along its sides the water glowed white, as if a swarm of fireflies or electric eels swam around it in the water. The submarine was maybe sixty feet long, and air bubbles arose from below and behind it. In the air there was a constant bubbly humming sound, and it was obvious that the humming was the sound of its engines, as if at any moment the submarine might slip beneath the surface of the ocean and disappear.

The path lay around the edge of the lake, ending at a point just beyond the pier against a sheer wall of ice. It was the only way in or out, which gave me a trapped feeling. Uncle Hedge stopped long before we got to the pier, and we stopped with him, and so did Reginald as soon as he knew we weren't following him any more.

"What's the plan, Reginald?" Uncle Hedge said to him. "Let's keep it simple."

"We parlay on board," Reginald said in his bubbly way. "Did you bring Basil's maps?"

"I said I would." He took the lead case out of his canvas bag and held it up to show he had them. "Have the Doctor send Lala out. She can return to the boat right now with my three. I need a word with him, and then I'll be on my way lickety split, and we can all go about our business. If he's not satisfied, then he's still got a hostage."

Reginald stood there regarding us through his faceplate. His eyes were weirdly enlarged by the glass, like the eyes of a deepwater fish. I could hear water swishing through the tubing and wheezing through the oxygenator at his belt. "The Doctor won't send her out," Reginald said. "You've got to come aboard."

"If it's the maps he's worried about, you can believe that I've got them right here in the box. I'm not fool enough to have come all this way without them. The bargain was clear. We trade Lala for the maps. I've got the maps. You tell him to send Lala out."

"He'll do things his way, not mine and not yours. You know that's how it is with him."

I could see that there was no chance of Uncle Hedge striking a bargain with Reginald Peach. Peach was too frightened of Dr. Frosticos. You could see it in his face. He looked like a man holding a burning stick of dynamite and wondering what to do with it. I looked at the submarine now, and I could see a face behind the glass of one of the big fisheye windows in the front. It was just a shadow, but I knew who it was.

"Head back to the boat," Uncle Hedge said to us, but none of us moved. "*Now*," he said. "Take the inflatable back across. Return for me or Lala when you see either of us on the beach."

We did as we were told, turning around and heading back up the path along the lake. Uncle Hedge went ahead with Reginald Peach. When we were near the place where the path entered the ice valley, I looked back. The two of them were just then stepping up onto the pier. I had a very bad feeling about things. Uncle Hedge had sent us away because he knew something was wrong, and something *was* wrong, and wronger every moment. There was a tiny vibration beneath my feet, as if the ice island was humming, and when I looked down at where the ocean lapped against the icy shore of the lake, I saw something that was very strange. Ocean water was flowing up over the shore now, as if the tide were coming in and the path would soon be submerged. But if the island were floating, it would rise with the tide. The tide wouldn't "come in." I had the oddest feeling of movement, a very definite feeling.

Perry and Brendan felt it too, because they stopped and looked down at the water, and then we all looked at each other. We *were* moving. The whole ice island was moving, although how fast it was moving and in what direction was impossible to say, because the ice cliffs and the pier and the submarine were all moving together. Tentacles of fog swirled in around the most distant of the ice cliffs now.

"Hurry!" Perry shouted, and we set out running, all of us knowing that if we were going to help Uncle Hedge and Lala we had to save ourselves, which meant getting back to the *Clematis* before we lost sight of it in the fog. When we ducked into the shadow of the little valley I glanced back again just in time to see Uncle Hedge and Reginald Peach disappearing into the door of the submarine. Uncle Hedge looked up just then, and I saw him move quickly back toward the pier, as if he saw that there was treachery. He raised the lead box as if to throw it into the ocean, but what happened next I can't say, because we were in the ice valley itself now, and we ducked around the first little turn and the lake was lost from view.

We had to slow up when we got to the chunk ice, but we scrambled and slid our way over it and through it, jamming our cleats against the big chunks and against the cliffs on either side, and kind of running up and over ice boulders that would have stopped us cold if we hadn't had the cleats. I banged my knee against an outcropping of ice and fell, and Brendan looked back and stopped and came running to help me up, and it slowed everybody down. But then we were scrambling along again, and to heck with being careful.

Suddenly right ahead of us there was sunlight glowing through the entrance to the valley, and in a moment we were out into that sunlight on the beach, and there was the inflatable right where we'd left it.

Except there was someone sitting in it now, waiting for us. It was Lord Wheyface the Creeper, as ugly as ever, and he was eating one of the sandwiches out of Charlie Slimmerman's tin picnic box. Where he had been hiding when we arrived on the island I can't say, probably in among the spires of ice, but it was him sure enough, and he had an evil smile on his face this time.

Chapter 12

The Fight on the Beach

The *Clematis* was a gray ghost, because the fog had closed in, and our sunny bit of ocean was getting smaller and smaller by the moment. Waves no longer ran up the beach, but rapidly fell away as the island picked up speed, moving across the water directly away from the *Clematis,* bound for who knew where, and us with it. The Creeper stepped out of the boat onto the ice now, reaching into his coat, and right then Brendan yelled, "Get him!" and without thinking we all went for him, with no one holding back, until we saw him draw a knife from within his jacket. We put on the brakes, then, and I was thankful for the ice cleats.

The Creeper would have been thankful for a pair of ice cleats, too, because he was wearing his boots, and he slipped now on the wet ice and threw his hands out to keep from falling. The knife flew out of his hand and skittered away. He lunged after it, trying to keep from slipping. It was a stupid thing to do, because if he had wanted to stop us from leaving all he would have had to do was push the inflatable out into the ocean and set it adrift, or stab it all over with the knife, and deflate it.

But he wanted the knife, and he surely didn't want us to have it, and in his wild hurry he slipped again. Brendan ran to the knife and snatched it up, and Perry ran past the Creeper to the inflatable, where he pulled one of the wooden oars out from under the thwarts. The Creeper was just then clambering to his feet again when Perry came up behind him, shouted "Melmoth!" and leveled a great blow at his back, knocking him forward. His feet went out from under him, and he slammed down onto the ice and slid nearly to the ocean, throwing his hands up to protect himself. Perry took another heavy swing at him, but the oar glanced off his shoulder and slipped out of Perry's hands and flew off into the water.

The fog closed in upon us then. A wash of mist swirled through, milky white, the last of the sun shining through it. I looked up and saw the tops of the ice cliffs disappear just like the *Clematis* had disappeared, and on the instant we were swallowed up too, the white mist turning to gray. The Creeper, who was just a few feet away, was a dark shadow, angling to cut Brendan off from the inflatable, but he was slipping and sliding on the wet ice. Brendan got there first, with me right behind him. Perry had pushed the inflatable into the water by now and climbed in, flopping down onto his rear end and pulling off his cleats so that they didn't stab things full of holes.

Brendan sort of bounced in over the side of the inflatable, the Creeper staggering forward now, maybe fifteen feet away, his arms out in front of him for balance. In another instant I was climbing into the boat, too, and yanking off my cleats, one of which I lost into the ocean because I was in such a terrible hurry. At that moment the Creeper caught up to us, looming up out of the fog. His face was petrified with rage. He took a desperate lunge at the boat as we drifted away, trying to throw himself aboard, grabbing hold of the motor so that the inflatable slewed about crazily. The ice island was rapidly leaving us behind now, and leaving the Creeper behind, too.

I crouched in the bow of the inflatable to stay out of the Creeper's reach, glad to see that he couldn't stand up in the deep water. Except then he began pulling himself up the back of the motor in order to boost himself in, and tried to get a foot on the propeller. Perry slipped the second oar from under the thwarts, and held it with both hands, aimed at the Creeper's forehead. "Let go *now*," Perry said, "while you can still swim to shore." He started to count to three, but the Creeper interrupted, calling him a skinny little something-or-other. Perry speared the end of the oar toward the Creeper's forehead, but then jerked it back before it struck him. The Creeper let go of the engine with one hand as if to grab the oar, throwing half his body up over the edge of the boat and catching hold of the painter, the piece of rope that ties the boat up to the dock.

Perry gave it to him for real now with the end of the oar, knocking him right in the chest, and the Creeper fell backward again, yanking down on the stern of the boat, which plunged downward, a great wash of ocean rolling in over the side. Perry lost his balance and teetered on one foot, dropping the second oar into the sea. I reached forward and grabbed Perry's jacket, seeing that the Creeper still had hold of the rope and was dragging himself forward again. But Brendan leaned out, holding the Creeper's knife now, and in an instant he had sawed through the painter, and the Creeper fell back and sank beneath the water, his arms flailing. Perry sat down hard on the thwart, and I went for the engine. It was time to go, plus some.

The Creeper was drifting away from us now, his hand holding onto the little severed piece of rope, which lay on the top of the water like an eel. He sank again momentarily and then beat his way to the surface, a good distance away. We heard him shout something I can't repeat. Then, just before he disappeared in the fog, I grabbed one of the canvas and foam lifesaving rings that was stowed along the edge of the boat and flung it hard over the side, not quite hitting the Creeper in the head with it. Then the fog was too thick to see.

◪

We motored away slowly in the direction that we had last seen the *Clematis,* or at least we hoped it was that direction. Brendan was shaking, and at first I thought he was just cold, but then I saw that he was scared, or something like it, and was staring out into the fog but not really looking at anything, holding the knife in his fist. He had defeated the Creeper, but he looked like the one who had been defeated. Even though it was the Creeper, you see, there was something awful about Brendan's cutting him loose from the boat—a man who couldn't swim, and who was wearing heavy boots and a greatcoat that might drag him to the bottom. Brendan bent down and picked up the picnic box, opened it, and put the knife inside. Then he sat and looked at his hand, which he opened and shut slowly.

"That was quick thinking with the life preserver," Perry said to me. "Maybe it'll change his attitude. Frosticos will pick him up in the submarine. You can count on that. When the Creeper doesn't bring us back, Frosticos will know something's wrong, and he'll go looking, and when the Creeper's not on the beach, they'll set out to hunt for him. He can't be seen above the water because of the fog, but below the water won't be a problem. No fog down there. All he has to do is stay afloat."

Brendan just shrugged at the end of Perry's little speech, but he seemed to be slightly less dismal. He didn't want to talk about it, though, and neither did I. Maybe it's shameful, but I didn't really *want* Perry to be right. I didn't want the Creeper dead, but I didn't want him alive either, and so I just shut up and let it be, and it took me some time before I was actually *glad* I threw the life vest. Soon we were distracted from all these thoughts anyway when we heard the ringing of a ship's bell.

Perry and I thought it sounded away to the left of us, off the port side, but Brendan said it had sounded like it had come from behind us, and so we compromised, and I turned us half around, all of us listening hard. There was nothing to orient us, though, and when we heard the bell again minutes later, it seemed to be off to starboard, farther away, and although I changed direction again, I didn't have any real hope. We sat in our little inflatable with the gray fog all around, and if it had been midnight it wouldn't have been any more lonesome and we wouldn't have been any more miserable.

Perry said that we should put on life vests ourselves, and so we did, and then we got situated around the boat so that our weight was evened out. I navigated us back and forth in big loopy curves, but slowly, so that we didn't run into anyone or anything, because we still couldn't see twenty feet ahead of us in the murk. Brendan has the loudest voice, and so he yelled "Ahoy!" at intervals, but we heard nothing in reply. After a while Perry took over the yelling, and then all three of us together, but after that we lost interest in it and fell silent.

Brendan was shivering badly now that the first excitement was over, because he had gotten wetter than the rest of us while trying to rescue the Creeper's knife. Perry dug out the emergency box from its little cabinet under the seat, and inside we found some very good things. There were rocket flares and a gun to shoot them into the air with, and there was a compass for finding directions, and there were blankets made out of a sort of aluminum foil that were folded up very small, and also there were yellow plastic rain ponchos. We all put on the ponchos, just to keep from soaking up more fog, and we opened one of the blankets and wrapped it around Brendan, who didn't argue with us.

There was drinking water, too, in packages, and there was a first aid kit and plastic bottles of red dye that you could squirt onto the surface of the ocean to make a big red splash of color that could be seen from a passing airplane. Except that a passing airplane couldn't see the ocean at all in a fog like this, even if you dyed it all the colors of the rainbow. The flare gun was similarly useless, and so was the compass. North might as well have been straight ahead. Maybe it was. The most useful thing was a sort of miniature foghorn that was operated by a can of compressed air. Brendan wanted to blast away with it right off, but we took another vote and agreed that we should wait until we heard a ship's bell again, and then blast away. Otherwise we might empty the can when there was no hope of being heard.

Perry passed me a ham sandwich, then, out of the lunch box, and I realized that I was hungry, which is very much better than realizing you're lost, at least it is if you have something to eat. Perry reminded us of what the Hungry Man said: "If I had me some ham, I'd make me a sandwich, if I had me some bread," and we all laughed at it, which was good. The Creeper had helped himself to our lunch, but there was still plenty left—ham sandwiches and slices of cold meat pie and dill pickles and cookies and bags of chips and a big thermos of hot chocolate that was still hot, which I can tell you is just the thing when you're lost in the fog. We started in with the sandwiches, leaving the meat pies until later.

Perry took the Creeper's knife back out of the lunch box and said that it belonged to Brendan now, that it was the spoils of war. It had a handle carved out of bone, and a wicked looking blade that was hidden in the handle, and when you pressed a button on the bottom of the handle the blade sprang straight out. Brendan said that he hoped Uncle Hedge would let him keep it, and that made me think of Uncle Hedge for the first time since I saw him standing on the pier, fixing to throw the iron-bound maps into the depths, and I believe that everyone else was thinking the same thing that I was—that we might never see him again at all. And just like that we were miserable.

We took a vote and decided to cut the engine to preserve fuel. It was pointless not to. We would feel like nitwits if we ran out of gas and then needed power, which we would if the ocean got rough, because it's better to move through the waves then to let them toss you around. And of course the oars were both lost, which was a bad thing, but not as bad as being caught by the Creeper, unless we were never found at all. In that case it wouldn't matter what was bad and what was worse. It would all turn out the same.

I put that thought out of my mind the best I could. We sat there drifting again, rising and falling over the long, low swells. The dark surface of the ocean was smooth, and there was no wind at all, thank goodness, because by now we were very cold indeed, and the fog was heavier and deeper and more lonesome than ever.

Chapter 13

Lost at Sea

Time passed. How much time? I don't know. None of us wore a watch. The world grew even dimmer. Night was coming on. We wrapped ourselves in the blankets and consulted the compass to get our minds off other things, and we guessed that we were drifting toward the northeast, or else we were drifting away from it—unless, of course, we were sitting dead still. We put the compass away. Perry started up a game of "Animal, Mineral, Vegetable," and that went well until Brendan used the word "doughnut" and said it was a mineral because it had sugar. I said it was a vegetable because it had flour, which is wheat, and anyway sugar comes from a vegetable, too, and one thing led to another and suddenly we were all talking about food, and whether it should be Animal, Mineral, Vegetable, Food, and whether something would count as food just because you ate it. Like let's say a frog eats a bug or a goat eats a piece of cardboard.

Then Perry said that he had read a book in which sailors, lost at sea in an open boat and starving to death, had eaten their belts and shoes, so those articles of clothing would have to count as food too.

"Sometimes sailors ate each other when they were starving," Brendan said morbidly.

"Starting with the youngest," Perry said, at which point I told them both to shut their gobs. We decided it was time for dinner, and Perry handed out the meat pies.

It was night almost before we knew it. The gray of the fog just got darker and darker, still hovering thick around us, and I sat for a long time staring at nothing, and wondering about mermaids, and whether there might be any thereabouts, and whether they really rescued poor lost mariners like in the stories. And then I must have fallen asleep, because the next thing I knew I was startled awake when Brendan yelled, "Look!"

The wind had come up, and the seas with it, and the first thing I thought was that we were capsizing, because the inflatable was bobbing up and down with the rising and falling of the seas. I found myself looking straight into a black wall of water looming above our heads, and then we rose on the swell as it passed beneath us. The water was ink-black—blacker than the night fog—but far down in the depths, off my side of the boat, there shone a pair of great, luminous eyes gazing up at us. And they were apparently growing, too, as they rose toward the surface, larger and larger, the glowing eyes of an enormous fish, a fish the size of a zeuglodon, or a vast great squid.

I thought of the creatures in the lake on the ice island. I could see the shape of this one now, not a squid but something more like an immense whale. Then more eyes winked on, as if there were several of the creatures all rising together, and into my mind came the thought that this was the end, and that we were going to be capsized and swallowed like Jonah. I held on tight to the thwarts, bubbles rushing up around the boat as we rose again on another swell. I saw that Brendan had the Creeper's knife open in his hand, although it looked pitifully small, but there was something about it that made it easier not to be afraid, for about a second, anyway.

Whatever it was in the water was now very near the surface, and I closed my eyes, the boat tilting and tilting until we were sliding backward down the face of a watery hillside.

I opened my eyes then, because scary or not I just had to see. There was a great agitation of the water, millions of bubbles churning up in a foamy rush, and the creature rose above the surface not twenty feet away, and just kept on rising, the seas flowing off its sides in a waterfall. We were all shouting like crazy now, and I slid down into the bottom of the boat, which had a couple of inches of very cold seawater sloshing around in it, although I didn't feel it at the time.

Then I saw what it was—the submarine, and not a sea creature at all. Its row of lights were glowing through the fog now. We could hear the hum of its engines, and we watched as it very slowly drew away from us, obviously not seeing us there in our little boat in that foggy darkness. Uncle Hedge must be somewhere aboard—I hoped he was—and Lala, and Reginald Peach, all bound for who-knows-where and, for the moment, only a biscuit-toss away.

"The horn!" Brendan shouted, and he took out the fog-horn can and popped loose a little plastic bit that protected the trigger. It let off a great blast that shocked us all it was so very loud. But the lights of the submarine continued to fade away through the mists, and so Brendan blasted another one, because all of us by then were cold and hungry and we would by far rather be prisoners and be warm aboard the submarine than be lost and eat our shoes.

But the lights winked out and the submarine vanished, just like the *Clematis* and the ice island had vanished. For a moment there was a sort of moonlike glow some ways off through the mists, but only for that moment, and then the night was as deep and dark as ever, and the humming of the engines died away into silence.

Brendan blasted the horn one last time, senselessly, because he was angry, and I said, "Don't waste it!" because I was angry too, although I don't know if I was angry at Brendan or at our losing our chance to be rescued. Then, in the moment of quiet that followed, just when I was feeling like it had been hope itself that had vanished in the fog, there was an answering horn, and close by, too. We waited, holding our breath and holding on even harder to the inflatable, because, as I said, the ocean had grown a little bit wild by then. The horn sounded once more, and Brendan answered with our horn, and the ship answered, closer now.

I started the engine and turned into the swell. The wind gusted, and the fog blew aside, and the night was suddenly sparklingly clear. The sky was alive with stars, and the moon shone down on the ocean in a long ivory road stretching toward the horizon. Not fifty yards away lay the *Clematis*, glowing with lights and with her big spotlight searching the sea. After a moment it shone right on us, blindingly, and we waved our hands and Brendan blew the horn again, half standing up and nearly pitching out of the boat as the searchlight moved on past. Then the light swung back toward us, and stayed there, and we all waved and shouted, just out of happiness, because there was really no more need for waving and shouting.

Brendan, I can tell you, was very much the hero, because he was the man with the horn. Perry said that it had been just like Rolland, I said I thought it had been, too, and so did Brendan, although I had no idea about Rolland, and I was pretty sure Brendan didn't either. Later Perry told me that Rolland was a great hero in the time of Charlemagne who blew on his horn so hard that blood flew out of his eyes and ears, which is either a very awful thing to contemplate or else a very ridiculous thing, depending. No part of Brendan's head had exploded, of course, and the air came from inside a can instead of from inside his lungs, but if he wanted to be Rolland it was fine with me, because his impetuous behavior had saved us from a hideous fate.

We bumped along over the choppy seas toward the *Clematis*, and before we knew it we were rescued, hauled aboard and safely back in our cabins and climbing out of our wet clothes. My hands were so frozen that it took me a long time just to work the buttons on my shirt, and my feet, which had gone numb, felt like they were on fire when they started to thaw out, and were still prickly and rubbery-feeling even a half hour later when we were all sitting in the saloon and telling Captain Sodbury what had happened to us—about the betrayal by Dr. Frosticos and about the Creeper, and how the ice island had seemed to be sailing away under its own power and the submarine with it.

Captain Sodbury said that he reckoned we could catch the ice island sometime tomorrow if we could fix the location. But then we told him that the submarine was now out in the open sea, that it had left its moorings on the island. The Captain said that was too bad, and there was no point in our asking why, because the answer was obvious. We ate again, hot food this time, roasted chicken and potatoes and any number of side dishes and a tub of ice cream. We were ravenously hungry despite the meat pie, but also very tired. Brendan fell asleep with his head on the table, and Charlie Slimmerman had to carry him to his bunk. As for me, I'd never been so worn out in all my life, and bed has never felt so good before or since.

◄

When we awoke the next day the morning was almost gone. Captain Sodbury said that there was nothing to do but wait. Uncle Hedge would pull something out of his hat, or we could call William Sodbury a grass-combing lubber on a lee shore. And it very nearly happened just like he said, except it wasn't Uncle Hedge who pulled it out of his hat, it was Reginald Peach, pulling it out of his seashell helmet. In any event, nobody had to call anybody a grass-combing lubber.

Reginald's message came in late that afternoon on the sub-lunar frequency. The submarine, he said, was bound for the west coast of England. That's the one thing that Reginald Peach told us that wasn't bubbleized into nonsense. He spoke for maybe fifteen seconds before the radio went dead, and that was that—no news of Uncle Hedge or Lala, just that the submarine was in a desperate hurry to get to somewhere called Morecambe Bay.

That bit of information made sense enough to Captain Sodbury, who said that environs of Morecambe Bay and Lake Windermere were "Lemuel Wattsbury's bailiwick." Frosticos used the Morecambe Sands as a sort of hideout, he said, which made no earthly sense to us until he told us about the Morecambe Sands themselves—about how the tide in the bay goes very far out, and exposes vast sand flats. The local people thereabouts call that part of the coast Sandylands, which sounds fun, but is actually deadly. You can walk out onto the sand flats, or even drive across them as a shortcut to some place farther down the coast or across the bay, but only if you're very careful or very stupid, because much of the sand is quicksand, and some of it is watery quicksand. All of it looks the same, though, and without a warning you find yourself sinking away into this watery sand, and in moments you're gone forever and you're living with the fishes.

In olden days the Morecambe Sands swallowed up whole carriages, horses and passengers and all, as well as any number of people who ventured out onto the sands to try to rescue the people who were being drawn under. If you're in a submarine, though, and if you have very carefully drawn charts, then sinking away out of sight in the watery sands mightn't be a bad thing, because there's nobody who would be foolish enough to try to find you. Captain Sodbury said that Dr. Frosticos had "gone to ground" there more than once, and was safe as a baby from anyone who might try to follow, and could make his way unseen into secret water-filled tunnels below the sands—tunnels that flowed out of Lake Windermere. And Lake Windermere, you'll maybe remember, is the ancestral home of the Peach family. Now it was our destination, too.

Chapter 14

St. George and the Dragon

That's how we came to find ourselves, the three of us and Hasbro along with Mr. Lemuel Wattsbury, motoring north toward Bowness-on-Windermere, the Wattsbury bailiwick. The Mermaid was sitting snugly in the trunk of the car and the trunk tied shut with a rope. Her exhibit box had been crated up into an even larger box, which said "Wheelchair" on the outside and "Manchester Theatre Company" below that. That was Charlie Slimmerman's idea—to disguise it.

Mr. Wattsbury and his wife Susan keep the St. George Lodge. Perhaps you can figure out from the name of their hotel that they're particular allies of Uncle Hedge and the Guild of St. George. But the Wattsburies aren't *officers* in the Guild— not like Uncle Hedge is an officer in the Guild. As is true of Mr. Vegeley, the Wattsburies are...helper-outers, you might say. Or perhaps you wouldn't. Mr. Wattsbury has a bald and very round head. Brendan said it looked like a pumpkin, but I don't think that's kind, and I told him so. Mr. Wattsbury is amazingly literary and has read nearly everything there is to read, most of it twice and some of it three times, just for good measure. He told us in strict confidence that armchairs agree with him, and that the more time he can spend in one, the better he feels. He also told us that he is most decidedly not a man of action, but had always wanted to be a "wit." He said that when he tries to be a man of action, like Uncle Hedge, he generally turns out to be a halfwit, and so he avoids it.

The St. George Lodge is ever so much nicer than American hotels, because it's really just a big house, and the Wattsburies live there the year round and are always bustling up and down stairs and cooking and watching the television, and taking care of the guests, and going into Windermere to the market for that evening's supper, and so you feel like company instead of like you're just passing through on your way to someplace else.

There's a window in the front of the lodge that's prodigiously old and is made of stained and leaded glass. On it there's a picture of St. George slaying the dragon and rescuing the princess. Perry said it was just like Michael the archangel striking down Lucifer during the war in heaven, except that Michael would have had angel wings and also in heaven there wasn't any princess, although I don't quite see why there shouldn't have been. Maybe she was home cooking and sewing. Mr. Wattsbury told us that when we set out to slay the dragon it's pretty much always the same thing, princess or no princess. I'm certain he's right, because it sounds so incredibly wise.

Just inside the door of the St. George, there's a cast iron Humpty Dumpty that's immensely heavy and is meant as a sort of greeter. It's amazingly like the Dumpty on the radio shed, and I told Mr. Wattsbury, so, and he said that he wasn't a bit surprised. I asked him if his was a talisman, but he said it was an egg man, which was meant to be funny, I'm sure.

Perry and Brendan and I took room 13, on the second floor, although we didn't end up in that room just by chance or because it's an auspicious number. We asked for that particular room after walking around the Lodge and having a good look at it and talking it over. We wanted a room that was strategic. One thing is that room 13 looks down onto the street, so that we could keep an eye out—for whom we didn't know, although it paid off later. Also, there's a tree outside the window with heavy branches that run out along the wall of the Lodge, past the far corner and shading the driveway. We discovered that if you open the window and step out onto the ledge, you can jump across onto one of the limbs just as easy as kiss my hand. (I borrowed that phrase from Mr. Wattsbury.) But you can't be afraid to really *jump*, because if you're timid about it you might not carry all the way across to the limb, and instead you'd fall into the shrubbery below.

Once you were out on the limb you could make your way to the driveway, and if there was a car there you could drop down onto the top of it and then climb down to the ground. Except when you did there might be someone inside the car, just getting ready to leave, but you didn't know that, and you might give them a nasty surprise and leave smeary footprints on the car, which are the kind of things that make people mad, especially the man and his wife from Michigan who are staying at the lodge and who call you a "little hoser." All of that not only makes you feel woeful, but it's counter-productive to being secretive.

So we found another route through the tree out to a low limb just above where the hedge meets the sidewalk. We could jump down easily from there, especially if we hung on and then dropped. From there we could cut straight across the street and into the pine woods on the farther side where there's a picket fence and a trail that winds down to the lakeside. The faithful Hasbro, alas, lived downstairs in the television room, because he's not the best stair climber and he's no good at all at climbing trees or at hanging and dropping.

The thing about Lake Windermere, which is in the north and west of England, is that in the summer it's full of boats, and even in the winter, in good weather, there are people out sailing or rowing, although when the holiday season is over, and the weather grows dark and cold, the lake is a much more lonesome place than in the summer. When we arrived the summer season hadn't started yet, and the weather was cool and rainy, not holiday weather at all. The lake is twelve miles from the top, at Ambleside, down to the bottom where it empties into the River Leven, which runs down into Morecambe Bay. There are great stretches of woods along the lake, some of them very old and dark, and here and there you'll find an ancient farmhouse and sheep pastures criss-crossed with rock walls.

We took Mr. Wattsbury's motor launch next day when we traveled down from Bowness to return the Mermaid to old Cardigan Peach. It's a wooden boat that goes very fast, although that day the lake was rough with wind waves, and going fast was a bad idea, because we bounced and smashed and it wasn't a fun sort of bouncing and smashing. Mr. Wattsbury let me drive the boat once we got going, which turned out to be useful practice. Several miles down the lake we passed a place where a creek comes rushing out of the woods on the west side. There was a farmhouse right there, that's nothing now but a broken down shack with an old millwheel that was turned by creek water a long time ago. Mr. Wattsbury pointed it out, and said that it was the uppermost edge of the Peach estate. The millwheel, over a century ago, had turned machinery that stamped out nails, and so the farm there was called Tenpenny Farm, because that was the size of one of the nails that they made.

Anyway, this creek, which is really a small river after a season of rains, carries a lot of silt and rock into the lake, which makes the bottom thereabouts shallow and treacherous. Mr. Wattsbury called it "shoal water" and he pointed out how the lake was all chopped up there, with the creek water running into the wind waves and all of it sort of turmoiling over the shallow bottom. I steered away from it, keeping to the deeper channel, but I made a point to remember it, which was easy because of the millwheel. If you want to be any kind of navigator at all, you have to know the shoreline and the bottom and the currents.

A quarter mile farther on we spotted the boathouse at Peach Hall. The manor itself can't be seen very well from the lake, because it's nearly hidden by trees in one of the more ancient sections of woods. The old stone boathouse sits right on the lake, and that's the first thing we saw from Mr. Wattsbury's motor launch. Through the trees beyond the boathouse I could see the maze hedge that encloses the ornamental water, which in this case means a pool full of waterweeds. Beyond the hedge lay Peach Hall, which was built out of stone and wood ages ago—time out of mind, Mr. Wattsbury told us.

We tied up to an iron ring set into the stone steps at the base of the boat dock. The dock had once been longer, but much of it had rotted, and there were several lone, shattered pilings sticking up out of the water. The boards at the end of the dock were broken and hanging, and in that weather, with the low sky and the deserted lake, the half-ruined dock made the whole world seem lonesome and abandoned. Of course I snapped a picture of the dock. I had been taking pictures of pretty much everything. I have to be fast, though, or Perry and Brendan will leave me behind. They're bored with my taking pictures, although they're not bored with looking at them later.

We left the Mermaid in the boat and followed Mr. Wattsbury along the path toward the manor. The path skirted the maze and then joined a road that curved around to our left and disappeared back into the forest. On ahead of us and to the right it became a broad driveway, paved with flat stones and running up toward a carriage house and then to the manor itself. There were weeds growing through the paving stones and dead leaves lying about, and it looked like ages since the last car had driven across it or since anyone had swept away the leaves.

The cornerstones of the manor house were perfectly enormous, and the old, weathered wooden beams must have been cut from entire trees they were so large. We walked up onto a wide porch with a piece of roof overhanging it. On the ground floor there were very high windows with diamond-shaped panes covered with old lacy curtains. It was dim inside, and I even when I squinted I could only make out the shadows of things—very large pieces of furniture, maybe. The name PEACH was carved deeply into the heavy door, and beneath it was an immense knocker made of greenish-colored bronze in the shape of a carp, with a heavy body and large scales and a hinge in its tail so you could use the tail to whack the door. Mr. Wattsbury banged away with it, but nobody answered, so he banged away again.

Beyond the curtains one of the shadows shifted and moved off, and I could hear the sound of tapping, like someone walking with a cane.

"He's in there," Mr. Wattsbury said.

"Why doesn't he answer?" Brendan asked.

"He's contemplating it. Old Cardigan Peach has lived a long, long time, and he's disinclined to hurry. His motto is 'measure twice, cut once'."

"Can we look around?" Brendan asked him. "Down along the lake? There might be a frog."

"Or a salamander," I said helpfully.

"Why not?" said Mr. Wattsbury, and then he told us not to go too far because it looked like bad weather was setting in.

We headed straight back down the path toward the maze, which is exactly what Brendan had in mind. The frog was just an excuse, as was the salamander. The maze isn't a big one, and it was built in such a way that if you trailed your right hand against the hedge, following every single blind alley, you could find your way to the center and then back out again. That was how we found the ornamental water—a circular pool, about waist-deep above ground, built from the same cut stones as the house. Ferns and mosses grew from between the stones, and water seeped out here and there, and in the depths of the pool there were the same waterweeds that grew in the lake. You couldn't see the bottom, though, because the pool seemed to be prodigiously deep.

Perry threw a dime into the center, and all of us leaned out over the rocks and watched it drift downward into the depths, shining for a few moments in the little bit of sunlight before it was swallowed up by darkness. In the instant before it winked out of sight, a big glittery fish swam out of the weeds near the surface and angled down into the deep water, flipping its tail and darting away after the dime. It had been a carp, I think—a great giant carp, gold and black and with enormous shining scales.

There was something troublingly dark and lonesome about the pool, and as the sky got cloudier it became even more forbidding and strange. It suddenly seemed like a good idea to walk back out to the path. Mr. Wattsbury wasn't on the front porch any longer, but had disappeared, perhaps into the manor itself. We made our way along the lake toward the boathouse, a long, low building, again built of stone, with great beams holding up the roof. The ends of the roof beams were carved into the likeness of mermaids that were very much worn away by time and weather. The door was made of heavy wooden boards banded in iron and arched on the top, and it was shut tight, with no pull or knob or anything on the outside, just smooth planks.

"We need to open it," Brendan said.

I wasn't so sure. "Maybe we should ask first," I said. "It's not our boathouse."

"Go ask," Brendan said. "Take your time."

And then right away, before I could think of something to say that would irritate Brendan, Perry said, "Let's try a window," and we all went back down along the side of the building, which was sheltered by overhanging trees. We saw right off that it was no use. The windows weren't the kind that opened, and also they were barred like a jail cell. Even if they weren't barred, they'd be too small to crawl through. We looked through them, trying to make things out in the dim interior. I saw an old rowing boat hanging on the far wall, and some oars beneath it, and ancient wooden planks and tools scattered on the ground. More windows looked out onto the lake from inside.

Dead center in the floor of the room was a shadowy square where there was nothing at all except darkness, exactly as if there were a hole there, a stairwell perhaps, or a ladder going down into a cellar or maybe leading to a tunnel to Peach Manor. From where we stood we could see that the boathouse door was fastened inside with an iron latch-and-lever contraption. There was no lock visible, but there was no need for one, because, like I said, there was no knob or anything on the outside. You could get out of the boathouse from the inside, but you couldn't get in from the outside. A door like that doesn't need a lock.

"Come on," Perry said, and all of us headed back around to the door. Perry bent over and had a look past the crack at the edge, where the latch was. Almost at once he said, "Look here!" and pointed to a place where the stone had chipped away over the years, or had *been* chipped away, maybe from strangers trying to get in. Because of the chipped-away stone you could see the bottom of the latch mechanism. And that meant that we might lift the lever, if only we had something to slide in underneath in order to press up on it.

We found a stick straightaway, but it was too thick, and wouldn't fit through the crack, and so we found another one that was thin enough but which broke. We needed something just right—thin but hard and tough, like a piece of steel. And we needed it quickly. I told myself that it wouldn't hurt to take a quick look inside, if only to find out where the stairs led.

"Maybe Mr. Wattsbury has a tool kit in the boat," Perry said. "We might find a fishing knife or something."

"A knife!" Brendan said, and he rooted in his jacket pocket and came up with the Creeper's knife, which you'll remember he had kept as a spoil of war. "Hah!" he said, and he snapped the blade out, slid it through the crack beneath the latch, and wiggled steadily up at it. The latch was maybe rusty or something, because it took a while, but then there was a scraping sound, a metallic click, and the door swung silently outward, nearly knocking into us. We stepped inside and stood there for a moment listening to the drops pattering on the roof, and the first thing that we noticed was that the dark square in the floor was a stone stairway just as we had guessed, a stairway which evidently descended to a level below the lake itself.

The tools and boards and such that lay on the ground were rusty and dirty from years of lying there, as if the boathouse hadn't been used for any purpose at all in half a century. There was an old, square, wooden mallet, and a saw blade with no handle, and some oarlocks, and a carving thingy with a curved blade, and some heavy, short nails that had square-shaped heads, as if they'd been stamped out down at Tenpenny Farm, which probably they had been.

Brendan straightaway started down the stairs. "Come on," he said peevishly, looking back at us, and Perry shrugged and followed him, and I followed Perry. On the stairs we could hear the sound of water lapping against stones, and there was a strong smell of the lake, very musty and weedy. It was quite dark, because the little bit of light through the doorway and the windows dimmed as you went down the steps.

"A lantern!" Brendan said.

And there *was* a lantern, right there in the wall, shoved into a niche, and beside it sat an old can with a rusty lid, full of what must have been lamp oil. We have oil lamps in Caspar, so lamps and lamp oil were nothing new to us. The lamp felt heavy, as if it was nearly full of oil already, so Brendan struck a match against the stone wall in order to light the wick. The match flashed so brightly that for an instant I saw farther down the stairs, which descended to another floor below. We had to strike three more matches before the moldy old lamp wick stayed lit, and even then it burned very low and smoky.

We started down, Perry first and Brendan following him and carrying the lantern. I came along last, and I had my hand on Brendan's shoulder. He would usually have shaken it off, because he doesn't want girls clutching at him (unless they're Lala Peach) but this time he didn't shake it off. The corners of the walls were cobwebby, and lake water leaked in between the cracks in the mortar, and the air smelled damp. Almost at once we came to some wooden doors set into the stone on the dry side of the stairs. They looked like cupboard doors, built of planks and studded with great, fat-headed nails and with heavy hinges that were blue-green with age.

Each of the doors, maybe a dozen of them, was carved with a name and a pair of dates, exactly as if they were tombstones. The dates went back to the 1600s.

"It's a sepulcher," Perry whispered, and the word gave me the creeps even more than the names and the dates did. I prefer my corpses to be buried, not put into cupboards. There was a death date of 1789 on one of them, Artemis John Peach, and another from 1867. This one had a woman's name on it—*Annabelle Crumpet-Peach.*

"She sounds like a pie," Brendan whispered, which should have been funny, except there were too many dead people nearby for us to be laughing.

"Let's go back," I said. "I don't think it's all that polite to be disturbing the dead."

"The dead don't care," Brendan told me. "That's why they call them dead." I gave him a dirty look, which he pretended to laugh at. When Perry started downward once again, I followed along, and we were soon at the very bottom of the stairs, where a tunnel stretched away into the darkness. We went on just a little farther, the lantern casting its glow onto the floor around us. Beyond that circle of lantern light, though, it was pitch dark. The air was cool and desperately silent, with only the sound of gurgling and dripping and the scrape of our shoes on the stones. A wall loomed out of the darkness, and the tunnel turned sharply to the right—in the direction of the manor house.

I stopped then, because a creepy feeling had come over me. I can't describe it to you, but there was something uncanny in the air, something that made me think of the dark depths of the pool in the hedge maze. I had the strange feeling that I stood at the edge of an immense dark place, like a big, shadowy room in a funhouse, and I didn't like the feeling at all. "I'm going back," I said.

"*Baby*," Brendan said, which was mean of him, and so I told him that being a baby was better than being stupid, and he said, "I'm not as stupid as you look," which he thinks is very clever, but is not.

"Just one peek around the corner," Perry said, "and then we'll all go back."

Brendan mumbled something disagreeable, but I said, "All right, but just one," and we all stepped forward and peered past the corner, holding the lantern out, and for the space of five seconds we stared straight ahead, our mouths hanging open with horrible surprise. The corridor was blocked by a heavy iron gate a few feet farther along. And sitting in front of the gate on a sort of bench built right into the stones of the wall was an enormous skeleton, staring straight back at us through black, sightless eyes.

Chapter 15

Patrick Cotter,
The Irish Giant

A nd I mean *enormous*—maybe eight or nine feet tall if he had stood up. He was sort of slumped forward, though, and peering straight at us, as if he wanted to see who it was that had disturbed his sleep.

Before any of us could say anything, or take another step closer even if we had wanted to, a shadow fell across the rock wall far down the tunnel—the shadow of someone carrying a lantern, coming in our direction, looming up silently. We saw that it was old Cardigan Peach in his black coat, just as he had looked in Lala's photo. He peered toward us from a distance of maybe fifty feet, and I could quite clearly hear him humming something, although it sounded more like a beehive than human humming. And then abruptly he vanished, as if his lantern had gone dark. Before we could turn to leave, poof!, there he was again, fifteen feet closer to us, coming along hummingly, and with his lamp lit again. He moved in a stuttery way, like an old jumpy filmstrip, and the humming was louder now, and it came to me that it was the same humming that I'd heard in the sea cave with Lala. There was the same water-on-rock smell, too, although mingled now with the burning oil smell of the lantern.

Then in the flicker of an eye Cardigan Peach stood right beyond the gate, still smiling, just a few feet from us, his eyes staring, holding up his lantern so that the light shone on his face. In that moment Brendan turned and pushed straight into me, and for another few seconds we were all shouting and pushing and trying to run. Then our lantern went out, and we were in darkness so black that I knew what it was like to be blind. I walked forward with my hands out straight until I reached a wall, and then followed it back to the stairs, which were just barely visible because of light from above. I leaped up them two at a time, looking behind me, expecting to see the illuminated face of Cardigan Peach following along behind me like a floating balloon.

Then it was light again. Perry and Brendan had stopped right ahead, and were stowing the lantern in its niche. Perry was staring upward, at a strangely-shaped shadow that was descending the stairs toward us, shuffling along. Mr. Wattsbury appeared just then, walking down backward and carrying one edge of the Mermaid's exhibit case. Evidently he had taken it out of the Manchester Theatre Company box. Behind him appeared, impossibly, old Cardigan Peach himself, looking toad-like and grim and wearing a tweed coat and heavy trousers—not the black suit he had been wearing only moments ago. And he wasn't holding a lantern, either, and he wasn't humming a tune. Perry and Brendan were looking very gawkily at him, and I suppose I was too.

They set the Mermaid's box down on the landing. "This is Mr. Cardigan Peach," Mr. Wattsbury said, dusting off his hands.

"At your service," he said, nodding to us.

I told him that I was Kathleen Perkins and was very glad to meet him, and Brendan and Perry said so, too, although of course they said their own names. Mr. Peach didn't look as terrifying as I had feared, but he was extremely amphibious, with a wide mouth and pale frog-like skin. His hands were partly webbed, too, like Lala's.

"Mr. Wattsbury has told me that you befriended Eulalie," he said. His voice was as strange as he was, very high and piping.

We nodded.

"I'd like to thank you for that. Perhaps some day I can return the favor."

I found myself thinking that he could do me the favor of coming home with me to meet Mr. Collier, just to make Mr. Collier's eyes shoot open.

"It's time to lay her to rest," he said to Mr. Wattsbury, and they went on down the stairs where Mr. Peach opened one of the sepulcher doors, revealing an empty stone cupboard inside. The two of them lifted the Mermaid into it. Mr. Peach took one last look at her, mumbled a few words under his breath, and then shut the door, entombing her in the darkness before turning around and ascending the stairs again. We followed silently up into the boathouse itself, where he paused by the windows, looking out onto the lake, which was dark now with the stormy weather. I was trying to think of some way of apologizing for having been meddling in the boathouse at all, but Mr. Peach was apparently sadly distracted, and so I stayed silent.

Presently there was the sound of bees droning on the still air again, very loud and insistent bees, although I couldn't see any bees flying around. I could smell rain on dry stone, and again I was swept up in the idea that I was caught up in a dream—someone else's dream. Mr. Peach was quite still now, as if he had wandered off into his own memory, just as Lala had done in the sea cave....

And now through the boathouse window the lake was impossibly bright and clear under a summer sun—no more clouds, no rain. There were trees standing as ever on the shore opposite, but they were green with leaves, and out from among the trees, as if it had been hidden in a little inlet, came a low wooden boat with two people in it, a man and a woman. The man was rowing, and so had his back to us, and she was dressed in a bright bonnet, very old fashioned, and was trailing her hand in the water. It was a perfectly golden afternoon, and the lake was as calm as water in a bathtub, and the only noise was the telltale droning of bees.

Abruptly the boat flitted closer to us, and then closer again, exactly as Cardigan Peach had done in the tunnel below. It was like turning the pages of a flipbook—all jumpy and hurried. I heard the woman's laughter, sounding as if it were falling out of the sky, and the man rowing turned his head and looked our way for a moment before turning back. The man was Cardigan Peach, but many, many years younger. And right then, when he looked back at us, the boat and the two people in it vanished. The sun disappeared, and the rain was falling, and it was no longer spring.

I was filled with the sadness of things passing away, of lost time, and although I wanted to say something to Mr. Peach, I couldn't, because I didn't know how to say it. He smiled at me, though, as if he knew my thoughts, and then turned toward the open door, going out into the weather without another word. I was very sure of something at that moment—that Cardigan Peach, and Lala too, have the power to make you see things that aren't there, things that are hidden within their own memories. Don't ask me how they do it. I don't know how. I can't explain it. They just do.

It began to rain harder, and the lake was gray and empty and choppy. We left straightaway, back down to the dock and into the boat and across the lake, bounding along with our jackets pulled over our heads to keep out the rain, and all fairly bursting with questions now that we were out of the spell of the boathouse and in the open air.

"You go first," Perry said to me.

"I'm second," Brendan said.

I thought for a moment and started boldly. "That looked like Mr. Peach in the rowboat on the lake," I said to Mr. Wattsbury. "And it was in a different season, and a long time ago. What's up with that?"

"What's up indeed," he said. "You might have asked Mr. Peach that question." He talked loudly in order to be heard above the sound of the motor.

"We saw Cardigan Peach down in the tunnel, carrying a lantern," Brendan told him. "But then he was upstairs, too. But he couldn't have gotten there ahead of us."

"He was even dressed differently," I said.

"There are many things about Cardigan Peach that are different," Mr. Wattsbury told us. "His clothes are the least of it."

"But when he was in the tunnel, was that really *him*?" Brendan asked.

"Ah, there you have me," said Mr. Wattsbury. "The tunnel under Peach Manor is a vast mystery. I know of nobody who has navigated it and returned to tell the tale."

"And what about the giant skeleton?" Perry asked.

"That I know something about," Mr. Wattsbury said, steering us into the channel opposite Tenpenny farm. "It's rumored to be the remains of Patrick Cotter, the Irish Giant, who died in Bristol two centuries past. He's known among the very few as 'the Guardian of the Gate'."

"What's down there?" Perry asked. "What's he guarding?"

"The Passage, apparently," said Mr. Wattsbury.

"But a passage to *where*?" Brendan asked, because of *course* there was a passage. We had seen it. The passage wasn't newsworthy.

"I can't say absolutely," Mr. Wattsbury said, "but it's rumored to lead to the realm of the Sleeper."

"*Him* again," I said, but then realized that I hadn't told either Perry or Brendan what I heard in the fog aboard the *Clematis*.

"Him, *who*?" Brendan asked. "What sleeper?"

"My knowledge gets a little thin there," Mr. Wattsbury said. "I've never even been inside the boathouse until today. Almost no one has, except the three of you, and you shouldn't have been. Not without asking."

We were suddenly very abashed, as you can imagine. Brendan mumbled something about having wanted to get in out of the rain, but it wasn't convincing, and we sped along in silence most of the way back up the lake, having lost our boldness when it came to asking questions.

There are some things I need to say that I haven't had a chance to yet, and they're answers more than questions. I'm going to say some of them now, if you don't mind. In that moment in the tunnel, when we were all gaping at Patrick Cotter's skeleton, just before we turned to run, I saw that there was a locking mechanism set in between two of his ribs—an iron plate with a big keyhole in it. That's one thing. The other thing is that the skeleton's right hand was missing. There were just the bones of his arm hanging straight down toward the floor. Uncle Hedge had told us that the Mermaid's key was a skeleton key. Where was it now? Very likely it was in the hands of Dr. Hilario Frosticos himself, safely hidden aboard the submarine deep beneath the Morecambe Sands. There on the boat I didn't say anything about Brendan's losing the key, because Brendan, like I already said, is sometimes sensitive, and I try to be sensitive to his sensitivity as long as it's sensible. I knew it was important, though—more important than we could have guessed, and of course Brendan knew it, too.

When we were drawing near to Bowness-on-Windermere, Mr. Wattsbury asked me, "Do you want to take her on in?" Of course I said I did. "Head for the petrol shed," he said, moving out of the way of the wheel and nodding at a wooden shed at the end of a short dock. But as we drew near we could see that the station was closed and the shutters had been drawn over the windows, and so I went on past, throttled back all the way into reverse to slow us down, and eased the launch into the boat slip, hardly bumping at all.

"Good job, Perkins!" Mr. Wattsbury told me, which made me feel particularly happy. We covered the launch with a canvas, but before we did, Mr. Wattsbury looked round-about to make sure we were unseen, and then held up the ignition key to the boat engine. He slipped it under the canvas and down behind the seat cushion of the front seat. "I never lose it this way," he said, and winked.

The water was empty, dark, and foreboding, and I was just telling myself that we were the last people out on the lake, when I saw that we weren't. A couple of hundred yards farther down, along a brushy stretch of shoreline, a boat was just putting out from a lonesome wooden pier. Its motor was nearly silent—I could just hear a bubbly whir on the air. There were two men in the boat, one of them with white hair that stood out like a tiny patch of snow in the twilight. The other man sat at the wheel, his face hidden behind an upturned coat collar and a hat pulled down over his forehead. As we started

our trek up the hill, they made a wide turn and headed for
the far shore, angling down the lake in the direction of Peach
Manor. But it was in the direction of a hundred other places,
too, and so I didn't give it another thought.

It was quiet in Bowness, the evening settling in and the
houses lamp-lit and cozy. The streets were almost deserted,
with only now and then someone hurrying along, holding
onto his hat and hunched over out of the drizzle. There
was smell of suppers cooking, and I was suddenly hungry
and anxious to be home. We had gotten to the St. George
and were turning up the walkway toward the lodge, when I
heard the sound of a motor coming down from the town of
Windermere, a town that's a mile up the road from Bowness.
Within moments a bus came looming out of the misty evening with the lights on inside, looking warm and cozy.

Inside the bus, wearing a hat and sitting very stiffly and
staring straight ahead, was Henrietta Peckworthy, and no
doubt about it.

The bus passed us, heading down toward the lakeside
where it went around a corner and out of sight.

Chapter 16

The Mysterious Stranger

The sight of Ms Peckworthy had flabbergasted us. Brendan couldn't speak, but gaped around, looking back down the road and then at Perry and me. Our nemesis had picked up our trail. But why? Surely not to recover the stolen notebook—unless Brendan had been right and there was something more to the notebook than we had thought. But even if that were true, the notebook was burned up anyway.

None of us spoke a word about it to Mr. Wattsbury, but followed him into the lodge, where Mrs. Wattsbury was putting dinner on the table—an enormous roast pork with potatoes and applesauce and bread and butter. I can't tell you whether the food was good or awful, because I didn't really taste it, but just pushed it around on my plate, dividing it up so that it looked like I was eating. Now and then I said, "Mmmm," in an appreciative way. Not ten minutes ago I was starved, but now I had lost my appetite. The mere sight of Ms Peckworthy can do that to you. She could hire herself out as a diet.

I saw that Brendan was secretly sliding pieces of food off his plate and onto a napkin in his lap, especially the vegetables. At home he slips outside and throws it all onto the roof, and for the next couple of days there are all manner of birds and animals up there. He says it's just like fairy food. The fairies love children for spilling food, because spilled food becomes the legal property of fairies as soon as it lands on the ground. And of course fairies aren't fond of adults, who get angry about spilled food and set about cleaning it up. Perry was eating everything on his plate, as he always does unless he's lost in contemplation. He eats very heartily, too, for a thin boy, and nods his head over his food, as if he has just heard some true thing. It's very difficult to watch him eat.

It seemed to take forever for dinner to be over, and then we helped Mrs. Wattsbury with the washing up, and so it was another half an hour before we had a chance to go up to our room to talk. "You children must be tired after your long day," Mrs. Wattsbury said to us before we headed toward the stairs.

We told her that she had hit the nail squarely on the head. "*Rem acu tetigisti*," Perry said, showing off. And Brendan pointed out that at home it was the middle of the night, and that he had half a mind to turn in, and I said I did too. But of course it was only *half* a mind—there was the other half.... The first thing Brendan did when we got up to the room was to open the window and pitch out the napkin full of cut-up food, which flew like a meteor straight into the neighbor's shrubbery. "A treat for the hedgehogs," he said.

"What do you think?" Perry asked, giving me a shrewd look.

"I *guess* hedgehogs would eat it," I told him, although I didn't really know what they ate—hedges, maybe. "It seems kind of like cannibalism, hedgehogs eating roast pork. Like with the starving sailors."

"Not *hedgehogs*," Perry said. "I mean, what about the appearance of Frau Peckworthy?"

"I'm wondering why she came all this way," I said. "It must be about us, but...."

"Maybe it's *not* about us," Brendan said hopefully. "Maybe she's just on a jolly holiday."

"Of *course* it's about us," Perry said. "By stealing the notebook you made it an *affaire d' honneur.*"

"It's always some kind of Frenchy thing with you, isn't it?" Brendan asked sulkily.

"Perry means that stealing the notebook made it personal," I said. "Peckworthy can't let us get away with it. It's an affair of honor now."

"Out of the frying pan and into the fire," Perry said.

"*I'll* give her a frying pan," Brendan said ridiculously, but then he looked sharply out the window, stood up, and drew the curtains almost shut. "Hark!" he said. "Here comes someone, and not just anyone, either."

Perry doused the lights so that we wouldn't be seen, and the three of us peered out past the curtain. A mysterious-looking man had come out of the trees on the opposite side of the street. He was quite small—not a midget of any variety, but small—dressed in dark clothes and with a cap pulled down over his eyes. He hesitated for a moment, looking back into the shadows as if he was worried that someone was following. He carried a stick in his hand, but it wasn't long enough to use as a walking stick—more the kind of stick you'd carry if you thought you might have to clobber someone. He stepped down into the street and hurried across, straight toward the door of the St. George. We lost sight of him, because our view was blocked by the tree outside the window and by the porch eaves, but we could hear him rapping on the door with the stick, and then there was the sound of the door opening.

We slipped out onto the landing at the top of the stairs and tiptoed down until we got halfway to the bottom. Any farther and they'd be able to see our feet, if they had happened to look. The small man was in the Wattsbury's parlor now, and even without getting close enough to be actually snooping, we could hear him talking quite clearly.

"Yes, sir," he was saying, "down at the old King's Owl. He was a strange customer, all right."

"How do you mean *strange*, Mr. Boskins?" Mr. Wattsbury asked.

"I mean he had a bloomin' great seashell on his head, didn't he? And it was full of water, and him breathing through a hose into his midsection."

Brendan squeezed my arm hard at that point, meaning it was Reginald Peach, but he didn't really need to, because it was moronically obvious.

"At the pub?" Mr. Wattsbury asked.

"Yes, sir. That is to say, not in the Owl itself, sir, but out by the wall opposite that runs down to the lake. Do you know the Old Door?"

"The wooden door in the wall?"

"That's it, sir. He said he'd be back at that very door in an hour if he could manage it, and would wait for you there. Them's his very words. *If* he could manage it. It didn't seem certain. If he could *not* manage it, then you were to play your part without a script, like the poet said."

"Tonight? An hour from *now*?"

"That's it, Mr. Wattsbury. He said it was now or never, that the others were going off to try the key. Mind you, I was specifically to say that they were going to '*try the key.*'"

They, I thought. Who else but Frosticos and the Creeper? So the Creeper was alive! It was the black cloud and the silver lining both together, although the lining was paper thin.

Mr. Wattsbury spoke again. "*Try the key*, do you say? This is all very mysterious, Mr. Boskins. I'm not fond of a mystery."

"Nor am I, sir. Nor was your man in the helmet. He seemed frightened nearly out of his wits, I'd say. I came here straight off. He give me five pound for my troubles, and in two minutes I mean to be up the road to spend my earnings. Don't look back, that's my motto."

"But was there any further message, Mr. Boskins? Anything besides the key and this clandestine meeting? Something I can make sense of?"

"I was to tell you, 'the girl is safe.'"

"And did he mention anyone named Hedgepeth?"

"Yes, indeed, sir. Hedgepeth ain't."

"Ain't what, Mr. Boskins?"

"Ain't safe, sir. Not by a long chalk. They're meaning to do him a mischief if the key ain't right. That's why it must be tonight that you act, while them others have gone down the lake. Your man in the helmet can't lift a finger to help or he'll catch it, and the little girl, too. He put the weight on you, sir, every last punctilio. It's up to you now. That was the last word from your man in the helmet."

It might have been a mystery to Mr. Wattsbury, but none of it was a mystery to *us*, I can tell you, and we lingered there halfway down the stairs for Mr. Boskins to leave, at which moment we would fill Mr. Wattsbury in on the details. And of course we would go with him to his meeting with Reginald at the Old Door.

If he wouldn't let us, we'd go without him.

But then the door to the St. George opened again—someone else coming in. We heard Mr. Wattsbury say, "May I help you madam?" and I thought that it was a woman wanting a room. But then, in the unmistakable voice of Ms Henrietta

Peckworthy, she said, "I've come to claim Toliver Hedgepeth's children."

I turned to Perry and Brendan, and Perry held his finger to his lips, and we got ready to listen again, although all of us were thinking the same thing, having to do with the tree outside the window and how long it would take to get down it.

Mr. Boskins had clammed up, and now he was taking his leave, and Mr. Wattsbury was saying, "Very good, Mr. Boskins, here's another fiver for your trouble," and Mr. Boskins said "Cheers," and the door opened and shut once again, and then Wattsbury said to Ms Peckworthy, "I'm afraid the children have been left in my charge, ma'am. The missus and I are entirely competent to care for them while their uncle is away."

"I have it on good authority that Mr. Hedgepeth is not 'away' as you put it, but is in fact either dead or missing. And on the basis of that information I have brought a legal document that allows me to take charge of the children on their aunt's behalf. *My heavens, it's that infernal dog!*"

She had apparently seen Hasbro and taken fright. "Bite her on the ankle!" I thought, trying to project it, although I shouldn't have. Not that Ms Peckworthy doesn't deserve to be bitten, but Hasbro shouldn't bite anyone simply for pleasure, his or ours.

"In fact Mr. Boskins has just been telling me that there's evidence Mr. Hedgepeth is very much alive, and is in fact right here in Bowness, Mrs....?"

"Peckworthy," she told him. "*Ms* Henrietta Peckworthy."

"Lemuel Wattsbury, ma'am, and *Mrs.* Wattsbury."

"Pleased," Mrs. Wattsbury said, although she didn't sound pleased, and who would be, talking to Ms Peckworthy?

"I'll just ask you to produce your evidence, if you don't mind, Mr. Wattsbury," Ms Peckworthy said. "Aunt Ricketts will insist upon it."

"Ricketts, ma'am? Are you referring to the bone disease?"

"I certainly am not, sir. I'm referring to the maternal aunt of those three wayward children. Your Mr. Boskins left in a *very* suspicious hurry with his fabulous evidence. Perhaps you'll want to call him back?"

"If you'd be kind enough to produce *your* document, Ms Peckworthy..."

We didn't stop to hear the rest, but went straight back up the stairs. The production of documents didn't interest us at the moment. The words, "They've gone down the lake," kept going around in my head, and I was certain that I had seen *them*—that the white-haired man in the boat at twilight must have been Hilario Frosticos and the dark-haired man had been the Creeper, setting out to "try the key," as Mr. Boskins had put it. But how long would it take them? They'd been gone for an hour at least.

We jammed pillows under the bedcovers, made the lumps look humanish, grabbed our jackets, turned out the lights, and went out through the window like the infamous criminal, one step ahead of the law.

Chapter 17

At the King's Owl

M r. Boskins had apparently come up through the woods, and so we would go down that same way toward the lake. The rain had stopped falling and the sky was halfway clear and very starry. The full moon was up bright enough to cast shadows, which was good, because it was the only light we had. I wish we could have brought Hasbro along. What you want on a dark night in the woods is a fearless dog with a good sniffer and sharp ears, but of course we couldn't have taken him, not without revealing what we were up to.

So we headed downhill one behind the other, trying not to slip on the wet leaves and mud, but moving just as fast as we could. It smelled piney and cold, and it was very quiet and pretty, with leafy moonlight on the forest floor in between the trees, and the wind just barely moving the branches. Twice the path forked, but we kept to the main path, because the others were covered with leaves that hadn't been trodden quite so flat, and so looked less traveled by.

Then just when I was beginning to wonder whether we had taken the wrong path after all, we saw a lighted window through the trees. The headlights of a car swung past some distance beyond that window—someone rounding a curve in the road, probably heading uphill from the lake. By dumb luck we had found our way to just exactly where we were supposed to be, the back of Mr. Boskins's pub, The King's Owl, although we didn't know that for sure until we came out of the trees and alongside the back wall, where we peered past the corner to see if the coast was clear, which it was.

We angled down along the wall, being deadly quiet and keeping to the shadows. At the front edge of the building we hunkered down very low and peered out again, ready to slip back into the darkness of the trees if we had to. But there was no one lurking, just the empty sidewalk. Over the pub door there was a sign of a very knowing owl, no doubt the King's owl, dressed in a nightshirt and cap and with its eyes half shut, as if it were thinking profound thoughts or were half asleep. He was holding a candle, and the flame of the candle had lit the point of his cloth sleeping-cap on fire, and so he looked considerably less profound than sleepy. Across the street there was a heavy stone wall, perhaps five feet high and wider than a sidewalk, with some low bushes along it. There was no sign of any "Old Door" although it might easily be hidden by shrubbery.

"What now?" Perry asked.

Indeed. It had seemed like a first rate idea to come down here, but we were early. Reginald Peach wouldn't be lurking in the bushes yet. A woman carrying a package stepped out of a shop down the way and walked toward us. She gave us the suspicious eye as she passed, and so Brendan said, "Pawn to king's bishop four," and Perry said, "Hah! Queen takes knight, check and mate," and the woman looked surprised and impressed that the two of them were playing mental chess, which actually they were not. It's the sort of thing they always make up when they want either to confound someone or to impress them.

"Let's go inside," Perry whispered. "We've come this far, we've got to see it through."

"*Can* we go in?" I asked. I had no idea. Did they let children into pubs?

"Let them try to stop us," Brendan said, getting all glary-eyed and puffed up.

I started to point out that they could stop us quite easily if they had a mind to, but Brendan pushed open the door of the pub and walked in, and so of course we followed. A bell jangled, and a woman looked up from behind a tall little table where she was reading a magazine and asked could she help us. I said the first thing that came into my head, which was that our mother and father were waiting for us, and I nodded at an arched doorway that led into a room full of tables. She nodded back at me and then looked down at what she had been reading without another word. We walked in through the arch.

The strangest thing happened to me then. I looked around the room, which was really quite nice, with a fireplace and dark wood paneling and stained glass windows and lots of old bric-a-brac, and for one strange moment I actually expected to see my mother and father. I don't know even now whether I *really* remember exactly what my father looked like, except for in old photos, but I pictured them quite clearly in my mind, the two of them sitting together at a table, looking up and smiling to see that it was us who had walked in.

I don't have to tell you how silly that was, or that something's being silly sometimes doesn't matter. You're crying over something, and someone says, "Oh, don't be silly," and it doesn't help at all, even if it's right. Being silly that way isn't a matter of *wanting* to. It's something that just happens. You wish it didn't, but it did, and that's that. Anyway, there were two tables with people at them. At one was an oldish couple with a sleeping bulldog at their feet, and at the other was a couple holding hands across a table and sort of blinking at each other.

Perry looked at me funny when we sat down, because he could see that I was crying now, just barely, and perhaps he could figure out why, although he didn't say anything. I wiped my eyes and looked at the bulldog, which was a great fat thing who reminded me of Hasbro. He opened his eyes just then and gave me a friendly look, and all at once I felt much better.

A girl came in through a swinging door from the kitchen and asked Perry, "What do you want, luv?" Brendan started snickering, and she smiled and winked at him, and he got embarrassed and quiet and began to study the menu very intently.

All three of us ordered a hot cocoa, although we really didn't want anything. When she left I took a good look around. You could see the ancient wooden timbers that the walls and ceilings were built out of, with the ivory-colored plaster in between, and wooden shelves here and there with pots and glasses and figurines and books on them. The fireplace was very high and wide and with a heavy black iron bar inside, which is called a hob and is meant to hold a kettle. The hob is the thing that a hobgoblin sits on—a hobgoblin being a fireplace goblin, which there would naturally be in an old pub like the King's Owl.

There was an interesting door in the wall near the far corner of the room—a small wooden door, but stoutly built and with a hammered copper crest on it and a great iron latch. It reminded me of the door in the boathouse at Peach Manor.

"What do you make of that?" I asked, nodding surreptitiously in that direction.

"I make a door of it," Brendan said.

"It's small," Perry said. "And that means it's old. People were smaller back in the day."

"Back in *which* day?" Brendan asked. "The day of the dwarf? Don't say something stupid and try to make it sound smart."

"It's true anyway," Perry said, "whether you think so or not. The average height of a man was eight inches shorter only a hundred years ago."

"Then how come Charlemagne was eight feet tall?" Brendan asked, "and could bend three horseshoes at once? And how about Goliath and Patrick Cotter?"

"The exception proves the rule," Perry told him, and Brendan began to say that it proved something else which wasn't flattering to Perry, when at that moment the very door itself opened, maybe two inches, and someone peered out. It was dark behind the door, and so you couldn't see a face, but the light from within the pub glinted off something that might have been a very large pair of spectacles, or might have been the faceplate of a seashell helmet. The door closed almost at once, but not quite all the way, then flew open an inch or so again, and then shut again hurriedly, exactly as if whoever was behind it had noticed us sitting there and done a double-take.

We sat there staring for a moment, and then I said, "Was that Reginald Peach?"

"Maybe," Perry said.

"It *was*," Brendan said. "I'm certain of it. I'm going to look."

But Perry and I wouldn't let him, and before he could argue with us the waitress came out with our cocoa, and we subtly plied her with questions. She revealed that the King's Owl was very old indeed, and had been old when her grandmother was a little girl, although her grandmother was a hundred years old and still lived in Bowness. Brendan asked if her old grandmother knew Mr. Cardigan Peach, who was a personal friend of ours, and the waitress stared at him for a moment as if she were just then seeing him for the first time. Believe it or not, her grandmother had been a housekeeper at Peach Manor nearly seventy-five years ago. More to the point, she and Cardigan Peach had been sweethearts, and used to go out rowing on the lake! The waitress, whose named turned out to be Betty, short for Betina, had been out there to the manor herself a few times when she was a child. Peach Manor, she said, was a repository of secrets, many deep and very dark secrets.

Perry said that yonder door in the wall had a Peach-like look to it, and he thought there might be a secret behind it, too. And she said that there was—and more than one secret. The pub had been built by the Peach family itself, back in the old lord-of-the-manor days, long before the time of Cardigan Peach and even before the time of his grandfather, back when the cellars were used to store contraband and were the hideout of smugglers.

"Smugglers!" Brendan said. "What kind of contraband?"

"Oh, I don't really know," she said. "Elephant tusks, I should think, and silk and whisky and bags of gold dust and silver and like that." Just then the bulldog people signaled to her, and she took their money and went off. The blinky couple had already gone, and except for us, the room was empty.

Brendan stood up and walked away from the table without looking back—straight to the door in the wall. He took hold of the handle, swung the door open a crack, peered in, waved for us to follow him, and then disappeared through it himself.

Chapter 18

Beyond the Secret Door

We followed him, because what else could we do? We closed the door behind us, leaving our hot cocoa untouched on the table. Betty would think we had bolted, which we had, at least for the moment.

"We didn't pay for our cocoa," I said when we were safely behind the door and groping along the dim passage.

"We didn't drink it," Brendan said.

"But we *ordered* it," I told him, "and so it's immoral not to pay, and leave a tip, too."

Perry said that Betty wouldn't mind our paying when we had a chance, and that we would leave her a double tip, even if we had to come back tomorrow. The walls of the hallway were built of stone, with an electric wire running down along the center of the rough wooden ceiling and a bare bulb casting a misty glow every ten feet or so. The floor stepped downward twice before it finally opened into a cellar, just as Betty had said, which was piled with wooden crates and old furniture and cleaning supplies and beer kegs and other pubbish whatnot.

At the opposite end of the room stood yet another door, which wouldn't open. It looked almost as if someone had tried to burn through it at some long-lost time in the past, because it was charred with black soot. The rocks that framed it were blackened, too, but burned or not the door was strong and tight. We knew it *had* to open, though, because whoever had looked out at us only a few minutes ago must have gone through it, and if he had gone through it, so could we.

Brendan jiggled the latch and tugged on it and pushed against the door with his shoulder. It sat there solidly, making a mockery of his efforts. Perhaps it was barred from the other side, too. Perhaps Peach had gone through it and dropped the bar in place.

"Rats," Brendan said, which is what he always says when he's disappointed, or, I guess, when he sees rats.

There was something about the blackened stones that made me wonder. One of them had the soot or smoke or whatever rubbed off, so that there was a ring of clean stone, maybe from hands touching it. It was set to the left of the door, along the edge—that is, about halfway up from the latch. I pushed on it hopefully, but nothing happened. Brendan and Perry very quickly caught on, however, and each of them had a go at it, but with no better luck. Then Perry picked up a piece of stick that was lying nearby and gave it a good hard shove. It pushed in maybe an inch, and there was a sound like a chain running across the edge of something hard, and a scraping noise from behind the door, which swung open now, revealing still another corridor. We stepped through and the door shut by itself behind us, and the stone moved back into its place.

There was an odd gurgling sound in the air now, like bubbles rising through water, and a weedy, musty smell that reminded me of the mud and water plants along the lake-shore below Peach Manor. There was a strange hissing noise, too, and a continual sighing, like the ocean rushing up onto a beach. We followed the tunnel downward in what turned out to be the direction of the lake, although we didn't know it at the time, and we passed another door, set into the side of the tunnel. There was night air blowing in under it, so it must have led outside. It was barred from the inside, too.

Perry lifted out the bar and laid it on the ground. "Just in case we have to leave fast," he said.

"Or if Mr. Wattsbury needs to get in," Brendan said, which I hadn't thought of.

We went on, farther into the depths of the cellar, slanting downhill all the while. It seemed to me that we must be very near the lake now. The thing about being underground, though, is that you can't know for sure, because direction doesn't really mean anything, just like on the open ocean. The sighing noise and the bubbling grew louder and louder until we got to yet another door, although this one was standing open. Beyond it was a high, long room that held enormous aquariums framed with rusting iron and with thick glass fronts. They stood floor to ceiling and glowed with light from overhead lamps. Tangles of driftwood rose from the sandy bottoms of the tanks, and long waterweeds waved in currents created by bubbles rising through the rocks and weeds and driftwood.

There was no one in the room, just fish in the aquariums, and so we tiptoed in, watching carefully for trouble and ready to run back down the corridor to the unlocked door. Some of the fish were perfectly immense—bubble-eyed goldfish as big as grapefruit, with orange and black scales that shimmered in the yellow light, and plate-shaped silver fish like automobile hubcaps and with wide, staring eyes. There were big, slow-moving, heavy-bodied fish that half swam and half floated, and fish the size of your hand, flat like a hand, too, that drifted like brown leaves with whirry little fins. The lamps overhead cast shifting shadows across the driftwood and waterweeds and sand so that the room was full of movement and staring eyes.

In a small room off to one side stood the aerating apparatus, a mechanical contraption that looked like something in a book by Jules Verne. There were four gigantic black rubber spheres or bladders inflated with air, being slowly smashed by heavy iron plates, one below and one above. The air was forced into hoses that snaked away into the aquariums, down through the water among the weeds and rock and driftwood, where the air was released and rose in bubbles, so that the water in the tanks was continually moving and the surface of the water was agitated.

One of the rubber bladders whooshed itself flat with a gasping sigh, and then the iron plate that had flattened it was hauled upward by a weighted rope hung from pulleys, and there was a sucking sound as air began to re-inflate the bladder, which swelled like a giant round lung until it was spherical again. Then the iron plate descended upon it once more and began to crush the air out of it—a perpetual motion of air coming in and air going out. From the look of it, it had been operating just that way for a hundred years.

We heard footfalls some distance away, and we hurriedly crossed the room and peered into a big hall-like room beyond. I thought it contained a single gigantic aquarium at first, an aquarium half as big as the room itself, but it wasn't an aquarium. It was a window that looked out beneath the surface of the lake, and beyond it, just visible in the moonlit water, lay the submarine of Dr. Hilario Frosticos, hovering a foot or so off the weedy bottom. There was a wide, spiral staircase in the room, leading, perhaps, to a secret entrance at the surface.

In front of the window, striding back and forth, was Reginald Peach. He moved his hands in jerky little movements, and he stopped and looked at his pocket watch and then stamped his foot, like he was worried, maybe angry. Clearly Mr. Wattsbury hadn't come, and that was ominous news, because it was time for him to be there.

Behind us, a corridor angled away like a hallway in a house. There were doors along it, two of them barred suspiciously on the outside. If Uncle Hedge was here, as he almost surely was, he was no doubt locked into one of those rooms. We left Reginald Peach to his fretting and went straight on down the hallway toward the two barred doors. The others didn't interest us. At the first door we slipped the bar out of its hangers, opened the door a foot, and looked in. Immediately someone stood up in the dark room—a shadow shaped just like Uncle Hedge. The shadow said, "You!" in a tone of vast surprise.

Chapter 19

The Battle in the Aquarium

Well it *was* us, and it was also Uncle Hedge, not dead or disappeared at all, and so much for Ms Peckworthy. He put his finger to his lips to quiet us down before we all started talking, and then he motioned us into the room. I pushed the door nearly shut, taking the wooden bar inside with us, so that no one would come along and lock us in. The first thing he said was that he had never in his life seen anyone more welcome than us, which made our sneaking out of the St. George worth it ten times over.

"We *must* find Lala," he told us. "And we must return with her to Peach Manor. She's desperate to save her father before the others find him, desperate enough to come all the way to California alone looking for the key. Without the key she couldn't get into the Passage, and without getting into the Passage, she couldn't rescue her father. There's more to it than that—even I don't know all of it—but you should understand that Lala was only doing what she thought she had to do. She *must* bring her father home before Dr. Frosticos and the Creeper find him. He's in some sort of terrible danger. What makes it difficult is that now they've got the key. We've *got* to recover it."

Our hearts sank, or at least mine did. "They've already taken the key and gone," I said. "Reginald sent Mr. Boskins to tell Mr. Wattsbury, and Mr. Wattsbury was to come round at nine o'clock sharp to meet Reginald, and to sort things out and rescue you and Lala while Dr. Frosticos and the Creeper were down the lake."

"But Mr. Wattsbury's not here yet," Perry said, "and we don't know why."

Uncle Hedge didn't look happy. After a moment of thinking, he said, "If the key fits, and I'm certain that it must, they might simply go on toward the Center, although navigating the Passage without Basil's maps would be a dangerous business unless they had a guide. And I know they don't have the maps, because I sank them. The only available guide is Lala. If they took her with them..."

"They didn't," I said. "I saw them on the lake, and it was just the two of them."

"And of course they *don't* have the key," Brendan said matter-of-factly, and with a great huge smile on his face. "They only *think* they have the key."

We all stared at him as if he had lost his mind. He said nothing more, letting his words sink in, glorying in them. And then very slowly he reached inside the neck of his shirt and drew out a silver chain with the Mermaid's key dangling at the end of it.

Right then I knew what he had done, because I was the only one who had seen him meddling with the Mermaid's box back home in the middle of the night. I had thought that he was trying to open it, but now I saw that he already *had* opened it and taken the key. I had caught him in the act of *closing the box back up.*

"I knew the key wasn't safe," Brendan said, "and so I opened the Mermaid's box and took it out, and put in that iron jailer's key that we had on the key ring in the toy box. I knew if the Creeper or someone tried to steal it, they wouldn't know the difference."

"Then Lala took the false key!" Perry said.

"That's right. And all of you blamed me. And you've kept on blaming me, and now you have to eat crow." Brendan said this to Perry and me, of course, since Uncle Hedge hadn't done any blaming and so didn't have to eat any crow.

"Hah!" Uncle Hedge said. "Foxed them, did you? Good. Keep it safe, Brendan. If something goes wrong, you three run for it, and don't look back. Helping Lala rescue her father is your mission, not rescuing me or Wattsbury or anyone else. We'll see to ourselves."

We agreed, but not happily, and then we all left the room in order to search for Lala, shutting the door behind us and barring it again for looks. There were three more doors remaining, all on the other side of the hallway, but of course we went for the barred door again, and sure enough Lala was behind it. When we opened it she stood up looking very wild and ferocious and ran straight at us, as if to take us by surprise and escape. But then she saw who we were, and she stopped short and burst into tears. As funny as it sounds, Brendan looked miserable when she started crying, although she had locked him into the closet and treated him shabbily and made a fool of him. That was a testimony to love, of course, but only a very brief testimony, because there was a loud shout from somewhere near by and the sound of running feet, followed by the crash and clang of something heavy hitting the floor.

Uncle Hedge shushed us and slowly opened the door in order to look out, just as the bent figure of a man staggered past down the corridor. He was clawing the air and sort of flopping along like...a fish out of water, I guess you could say, although perhaps it wouldn't be altogether nice, because it was

Reginald Peach, without his seashell helmet and canister. He uttered a long, inhuman, burbling cry that sent a chill straight through me. *They're back!* I thought. Frosticos and the Creeper had done this terrible thing to Reginald Peach because he had helped us. But they would only know he had helped us if Mr. Wattsbury had come. Whatever that meant, it wasn't good.

Uncle Hedge stepped out into the hallway, and we followed. Reginald collapsed with his eyes rolled up into his head and making awful gasping noises. It came to me that we might try artificial respiration, but then I knew that wouldn't help, being that he was a human fish with gills instead of lungs, and was drowning in the air. Lala pushed out behind us and said, "Put him into the water!" which of course was the only sensible thing to do.

We hoisted him up and half walked, half carried him out into the room full of aquariums, looking around for the Creeper or Frosticos, who were nowhere to be seen, at least for the moment. Uncle Hedge lifted Reginald's hands so that he could grip the top edge of one of the big aquariums, but he hung there like a man half dead, his head lolling back onto his shoulders, unable to help himself.

"Reginald!" Uncle Hedge shouted. "You've got to hoist yourself up, man!

"*Climb*, Uncle Reginald!" Lala said, and we all latched onto his legs and under his feet and heaved him upward, saying, "Climb! Climb!" Reginald seemed to recover his senses for a moment, and to grasp what we were trying to do, and he blinked around, goggling at us, his head lolling pitifully. He tried to pull himself upward now, making a last, desperate effort to save himself.

"Heave-ho now!" Uncle Hedge cried, and we grabbed Reginald by the ankles and feet and heaved him upward like a sack of potatoes or hamsters or some other weighty thing.

Reginald teetered against the edge for a moment before toppling into the aquarium, slopping out gallons of water like Archimedes climbing into the bathtub.

"What a great deal of tumult," a voice said from behind us, very flat, almost machine-like. It wasn't the Creeper. It was a voice I had never heard before, and it was worse by far than the Creeper's. If you can imagine the voice of a dead man…but you can't—not until you've heard it.

Reginald was floating in the aquarium among the frightened fish, his feet hidden in the water plants and his coat sort of billowing out around him in the bubbles. He wasn't dying anymore, though, and that was good. What was not good is that the man who had spoken was Dr. Hilario Frosticos. He was pure white, like laundry detergent. He wasn't any age you could identify, but looked as if he might be a corpse, kept alive by artificial means, or as if perhaps had died and then been brought back to life, but only after a fairly rotten week had passed. There was something more to him—something evil. You could feel it more than you could see it. He made me think of a poisonous white spider, except that spiders can't help being what they are.

Beside him stood the Creeper, whose hand was in his coat. Clearly he had a hidden weapon, probably one of his knives, and I was afraid that Brendan would haul out his own knife, which would be an utter stupidity. Brendan, however, had a remote look on his face. He was thinking about something, but it wasn't knives.

"Reginald has betrayed us, Hedgepeth," Frosticos said. "And you've betrayed us. Betrayal seems to be in the air. I rather expected it from Reginald, who summoned your man Wattsbury when we left for the Manor to try the key, but I hardly expected it from you. Not when there were young lives at stake."

"I haven't betrayed anyone," Uncle Hedge said evenly. "I assumed that the key was genuine, as did Lala. Where's Lemuel Wattsbury?"

"Discommoded, I fear. Knocked on the head when he was coming in through the Old Door on his way to meet with our fishy friend here." He gestured at Reginald, who was probably safer now than we were.

Frosticos reached into his coat pocket then and took out a heavy iron key—the jailer key from our toy box.

"Useless," Frosticos said, and he tossed the key into the aquarium, where it sank to the bottom. "I'll take the authentic key, and I'll take it now."

"I'm afraid I can't help you," Uncle Hedge said. "I don't have it."

"Nonsense. You wouldn't have come all this way without it. I'm a patient man, Hedgepeth, but I won't put up with someone who plays the fool. That's not an instrument I've ever been able to abide."

I saw Lala mouth something to Brendan, who crossed his arms over his chest now, as if he had something to hide, which he did. His jacket was open, and the front of his shirt had been pushed all over the place in our struggle with Reginald. One of the buttons had come loose, and you could see the silver chain and the top of the key.

"For the sake of the children, then, Hedgepeth," Frosticos said, glancing our way.

"I tell you that I don't have the key," Uncle Hedge said, but Frosticos wasn't paying attention. He was looking straight at Brendan now, and he had a calculating look on his face. Somehow he knew what Brendan was hiding.

What happened next happened very quickly. Lala said "Now!" and she turned and ran, straight toward the spiral stairway and the window on the lake. At the very same moment, Brendan yanked the key off his neck, breaking the chain, and threw it hard at Lala, and then spun around and bolted past the Creeper and Frosticos, back toward the pub, running fast.

The Creeper drew his knife, and I believe he would have thrown it at Brendan out of anger, but before he could, Uncle Hedge hit him hard on the side of the head, and the Creeper staggered backward, waving the knife in the air. He got his balance soon enough, but by then Brendan was out of sight.

"Don't bother with the boy," Frosticos said. "He can't go far. It's the Peach girl we'll need!"

The Creeper strode away toward the stairs, where there was a small splash beyond the window. It was too late for him to do anything at all, unless he could swim like a fish. Lala appeared beyond the glass, her hair floating in a sort of halo around her head. She peered in at us for one long moment, showing us that she had the key, the broken chain still hanging from it, and then she turned around and began to swim away under water, disappearing out of the circle of light and into the darkness of the lake.

It was then that Brendan reappeared, walking back toward us. Behind him strode Ms Peckworthy, holding her umbrella as if she meant to poke someone in the eye, and with her mouth all pickled up with determination. Mr. Wattsbury lurched along behind her, with blood running out of his hair so that he looked like a gory apparition, not at all the bookish man in the armchair. It looked like a standoff to me, but it didn't stay that way long, because Lala Peach had finally gotten what she had gone to California to get. But Dr. Frosticos had nothing, not the key, not the maps, not Lala.

Chapter 20

Death or Glory

Ms Peckworthy stared at the lot of us for a long moment, apparently recognizing the Creeper, either as the mysterious, lurking, Lala-kidnapping stranger from back home, or as a partner. You couldn't tell which. Then she spotted Reginald Peach, who appeared to be an aquarium exhibit, and the look in her eyes made it seem as if every strange and awful thing she had ever imagined had finally come true. She opened her mouth as if to say something, but she never had a chance.

"Death or glory!" Mr. Wattsbury shouted suddenly, breaking the astonished silence, and he hurled himself in the direction of the Creeper like a wild man. Uncle Hedge shouted, "Run!" (meaning us) and he charged forward at the same moment and plowed into Frosticos. The momentum carried them both forward so that they slammed into the Creeper just as Wattsbury got to him, and they all went down in a heap with Ms Peckworthy wading in to beat all of them to pieces with her umbrella. Perry grabbed my hand and we were running, back up the corridor in the direction of the pub, with Brendan just ahead of us. Before we knew it we were at the door in the tunnel wall, the Old Door, which stood wide open now.

There was a warning shout from behind us, and a shattering crash, and someone shouted, "Look out for the knife!"

"I'm going back," I said, and I meant it. I wasn't going to leave Uncle Hedge behind, not again.

"We've *got* to find Lala," Perry gasped at me. "That's orders."

"How can we find Lala when she already swam away?" I asked.

"We'll take Wattsbury's boat," Brendan said, "We'll search the lake!"

"Latch on!" Perry shouted, glancing at Brendan, and both of them grabbed me, one on either wrist, and dragged me through the door whether I wanted to or not, out into a shrubbery of willows that hid everything from view except the sky. We could hear the barking of a dog, and straight off I knew it was Hasbro, somewhere nearby. We shouldered our way through the willows, only to discover that we were very near the water. Hasbro was tied up to a post where Mr. Wattsbury had apparently left him, and he was glad to see us and to be untied.

There was an old wooden dock where the boat was moored that I had seen out on the lake earlier in the evening. At the shore-end of the dock there was a small shack, which hid the stairway and the outside entrance into the aquarium. Within the lake itself there was a patch of water illuminated from underneath, the light glowing out through the big window, and in the light we could see the submarine lying ghostly and still, nearly on the lake bottom. Just the top of it emerged from the water alongside the dock.

"We've got to scuttle their boat," Brendan said, and he was off and running down the dock with us following. But how would we scuttle it? I had no idea. Then I saw that we didn't need to. The key was in the ignition. They had simply left it there, as if they had thought they were coming right back. With that thought in my mind, I snatched the key out, stomped on the plastic float that was chained to it, and pitched it straight into the lake, where they'd never find it. We couldn't do anything about the submarine, of course, and so it was time to search for Lala, except there she was, popping up out of the water near the end of the dock where there was a wooden ladder. She climbed out while Hasbro dashed back and forth, barking out a welcome. Then she walked straight up to Brendan and kissed him right on the lips!

I didn't laugh, because it wasn't funny. Okay, it *was* funny, because of the silly look on his face. But more than that it was Brendan saving the day. And anyway there was no time for laughing or for anything like it. We were running again, all five of us, along the shore, and then up onto the walkway that edges the lake, past a crowd of geese that were hunkered down for the night, and a man asleep on a bench under a big coat. We ducked around the ticket house where you pay for lake tours, and out onto the docks where we whipped the canvas cover from the top of Mr. Wattsbury's boat and crammed it in behind the seats. Brendan fished out the hidden ignition key, and I started up the engine, and in seconds we had backed out of the slip and were heading out across the moonlit lake, which was so smooth now that it felt almost as if we were flying.

But flying where?—to Peach Manor, of course, but what then?

"Uncle Hedge says we're supposed to help you," I shouted to Lala, who must have been freezing in her thin dress, given that she was all wet. I pulled off my jacket and handed it to her, and I could see that Brendan wished he had given her his jacket. Then Brendan gave his jacket to me, and I took it and said thanks. And then Lala traded me my jacket for

Brendan's. Brendan can be very gallant when he tries, and Lala knew just how to make him try.

"What's our mission, Peach?" Perry asked.

She held up the Mermaid's key, which she was gripping very tightly. "We have to rescue my father before he wakes up," she said, which still made not a single bit of sense to me, because it seemed to me that if her father waked up, he could rescue himself. Boy did I turn out to be wrong. But there was nothing to do except race the four miles down the lake, which reflected a glowing avenue of moonlight, straight and true. Hasbro climbed up onto the bow like a doggy figurehead, and the happy thought came into my head that we had gotten clean away.

But that kind of thought is like an unlucky penny, because just when it turns up, things are often about to go bad.

"Look!" shouted Brendan, and he pointed back up the lake in the direction we'd come. There was this strange bulge in the water, moving straight down along the center of the lake in the moonlight, right in our own wake, like a half-submerged alligator, and then the submarine itself rose partway out of the water, pursuing us, and maybe a quarter of a mile behind.

"It's the submarine!" Brendan yelled unnecessarily.

And Perry said, "Krikey! Step on it, Perkins!"

Light shone through the porthole windows in the front of the sub, and water swept backward in waves along its sides. I thought about Uncle Hedge and Mr. Wattsbury and Reginald Peach. Something had obviously gone very badly wrong if Frosticos and the Creeper had gotten away so quickly, but it wouldn't help to think about it now, because we were in real trouble if they caught us. It was moving worryingly fast, and there was no way we would have time to tie up our boat and break into the boathouse and light the lantern and unlock

Patrick Cotter's door and lock it back up again. By that time Frosticos and the Creeper could have stopped to smoke a cigar and play a hand of cards, and still they would have caught us in the end, after we'd done all the work.

Lala was looking back at the submarine with pure, frightened desperation in her eyes. I pushed the throttle forward so that the boat almost flew out of the water.

"We're gaining on them now!" Brendan shouted hopefully, and we shot down the center of the lake, throwing long streamers of moonlit water behind us, going so fast that the sound of the engine seemed to fly away backward with the spray. We were gaining, but not enough, and couldn't gain enough even if we really could fly.

I saw the old mill at Tenpenny Farm up ahead, and the churning shoal water where the creek ran into the lake, and I remembered something Uncle Hedge had read to us once— that the race isn't always to the swift, but that time and chance happeneth to us all. Right now, swift wasn't enough to win the race, but if I could make something happeneth to the submarine...

I backed off on the throttle, slowing down, and I steered the launch toward the mill, which was coming up fast.

"What?" Brendan shouted, giving me a furious look. "We've got them! *Floor* it, Perkins! For Pete's sake!"

"Never mind Pete!" I shouted back, which wasn't all that clever, and I slowed down even more, looking back over my shoulder. The submarine was following! It was winner-take-all, and they didn't mean to lose.

We moved more slowly yet along the very edge of the shoal water, because it was dangerous territory, even though the boat didn't draw very much water. Also, I wanted to let the submarine come up to us. I was betting everything on their following right behind. I glanced back, and they were close, scary close. You could see through the portholes into the interior, and there was no mistaking the Creeper and Frosticos, staring straight at us. But the thing that nearly made me fall over the side and drown was the third passenger, standing between them.

It was Ms Peckworthy, and not a doubt about it. She had betrayed us back at the aquarium! Stinking old Peckworthy! Brendan had been right again. Did she even *know* my Aunt Ricketts?

"She's struck!" Perry shouted, and I turned around so fast to look that I forgot what I was doing and jerked the wheel sharp to port so that our wake caught up to us and sloshed right over the side of the boat and got Brendan's shoes wet. He didn't even look down, because he was gaping back at the submarine, which was tilted up out of the water and stopped dead. They had run straight up onto the shoal! They hadn't slowed down, the greedy slugs, but had thought they'd got us at last, and now they were run aground!

There was no time to shout insults, and I turned back out toward the middle of the lake and hit the throttle again, and in three seconds we were flying along like crazy. Perry said, "Nice work, Perkins," and Lala clapped her hands, and I was immensely glad, which was tempting luck again.

There was a sort of coughing sound, and the launch gave a shudder and a jerk, sprinted forward again, and then shuddered and jerked a second time. I turned hard toward shore and looked at the fuel gauge, which showed empty, dead empty, and I remembered then that Mr. Wattsbury had told me to pull up alongside the petrol station when we'd come in earlier, but it had been closed.

"We're out of gas!" I shouted.

Lala stood up, ready to leap out into the water and swim, but she sat back down hard when I pushed the throttle full forward, saying a little prayer that there was a thimbleful of gas left in the line. There was, and we shot ahead again, straight at the beach. The engine coughed one last time and cut out, and there was a sudden perfect silence as we flew forward over the last ten yards of open water, and with no way to slow the boat down. "Hold on!" I shouted, and everyone did, and we drove up onto the shore and stopped dead in the weedy sand. Hasbro shot off the front of the boat like a meteor, landing in the weeds and springing up happily, as if it was great fun.

There was no time to worry about Mr. Wattsbury's motor launch. It was high and dry anyway, and could take care of itself. We jumped out and ran for it, following Lala and Hasbro, who led us down along the shore toward the woods. I took one last look back, and I could see that the submarine was still stuck fast onto the shoal, its headlight shining into the sky. There was a furious bubbly buzzing out on the lake, and the moonlight glowed on the water roiling up around the stern of the submarine as they tried in vain to back off into deeper water. Then we plunged into the darkness of the woods, running for all our might along dark paths.

Chapter 21

Skeleton Key

We were suddenly in the open again, with the starry sky above us and the woods behind. There in front of us was the shadowy maze hedge and off to the left lay lake and the dark boathouse. In an instant we were there at the door, breathing hard while Brendan fumbled with the latch, trying to wedge it open with the Creeper's knife. I said, "Hurry!" but he was already hurrying just as hurriedly as he could. Lala stood there clutching the skeleton key and looking anxiously out at the lake and back toward the woods.

"Let *me* try!" Perry said, but just then the door swung open and we all jumped back out of the way before pushing and shoving each other through. We shut the door, making sure it was latched and wishing there was some way to lock it or wedge it shut. The Creeper and Frosticos had gotten in earlier, and they would do it again. But we couldn't stop them—couldn't even try without wasting time. It was better to go on.

The interior of the boathouse was dark, with just the faintest glow of moonlight through the windows, but we found the lantern right enough, although we had to take it back upstairs to the window in order to have enough moonlight to see by. Perry twisted the lid off the can of oil, opened the oil chamber in the lantern, and carefully poured it full. It lit right away this time, first match, and Perry adjusted the wick so that it was bright and not smoky.

We started downward again, taking the oil and the matches with us, and found Patrick Cotter sitting as ever. Lala very boldly slid the key into the keyhole between his ribs and tried to turn it. It wouldn't budge. She twisted at it, sliding it out a little and trying again, then jiggling it, but it was no use.

"Maybe it's rusted shut," I said. "Try some oil." Lala held out the key, and Perry dribbled lamp oil on it, and Lala tried it again. There was a little snapping sound, the key popped another quarter inch into the lock, and there was a ratchety noise, exactly like the turning of the mechanism in the Mermaid's box. The skeleton's handless arm jerked suddenly upward, knocking Lala on the chin with its wrist bone.

She said, "Ow!" and stepped back, and the four of us stood watching to see what the skeleton would do.

Where the hand had been severed from the wrist there was a flat metal disk with a keyhole-shaped hole in it. The metal disk was screwed tight to the cut-off wrist bone. The arm moved inward toward the skeleton's chest now, and then the bones in his forearm swiveled back and forth, as if it were trying to turn the key, except that without a hand it couldn't turn anything at all. It finished its turning and swiveling, and the arm ratcheted back again and dropped toward the floor, and the skeleton sat there as ever, probably thinking that it had done its job.

The truth came to me like a poke in the eye. "It's Patrick Cotter's hand in the Mermaid's box," I said. "He needs his hand!"

You'll say that I should have figured it out sooner, that I should have known that the skeleton would want his hand.

But I hadn't, and neither had Lala or Perry or Brendan. But now it was clear to all of us, and we started back up the tunnel toward the stairs.

"What will we *do*?" Lala asked, because obviously she didn't know that the Mermaid had been stowed in her sepulcher.

By then we were already there, and Perry had the door open in a trice. Lala said, "Ah!" very happily. Perry went to work on the sliding pieces of the puzzle box, and Brendan explained to Lala that we had hidden the Mermaid in the sepulcher earlier, which wasn't precisely true, although there was no point in correcting him.

Soon the Mermaid was going through her revolutions, with all of the mechanism's metallic noises. The hand slid out and opened up, and of course it was empty. Perry tried to take it out of the box, but it wouldn't come, and I was afraid that in his hurry to get it out he would break it, but he didn't. He slid his own hand, which is very skinny, in behind the skeleton hand, fiddled with something, frowned and fiddled again, and the hand came loose. He turned it around, and in the back was a little key-shaped piece of metal that had locked it into the Mermaid's box, and which would fit perfectly into the keyhole in the metal disk fastened to Patrick Cotter's wrist bone.

We picked up the lantern and headed back down the stairs, careful this time when we got to the skeleton, not rushing Perry as he fitted the hand carefully onto its arm. A lost finger bone might spell failure or delay, and we couldn't afford either one. I listened hard for sounds from above, expecting to hear them coming through the door at any moment. Instead there was the satisfying sound of a click as the hand locked into place, and Lala put the key into the keyhole again, and we all held our breath.

Patrick Cotter repeated his movements, but he had a hand now, and he reached up and grasped the key and turned it himself, just like that. There was the sound of ratcheting in the walls again, but this time Patrick Cotter stood up from his stone bench—right up onto his feet, his head maybe an inch from the stone ceiling. We all trod backward, getting out of his way.

Dust fell from his joints and bones. His teeth clacked together like he was trying his jaw out for the first time in an age. He looked down at his hands, although what I mean by "looked" I don't know, because he hadn't any eyes. His skull swiveled on his neck, as if he was trying to recall how he'd come to be here, in this tunnel, and under these strange circumstances. His mouth opened and shut, and I was certain that he was going to speak, and I wondered what marvelous thing he would have to say after all those years of sitting and waiting and thinking the thoughts that a skeleton thinks.

But he didn't speak. He simply fell to pieces. He shivered like a person with a bad chill, and he collapsed downward in a clacking heap of loose bones, as if he had been poured out of a sack. His skull bounced away down the tunnel, and the locking mechanism in his rib cage clanked to the stones of the floor with the key still in it.

We stood there gaping with disbelief. Patrick Cotter had waited patiently through the long years of darkness, only to stand up and fall to bits when his heroic moment finally arrived. What a tremendous disappointment, I thought, feeling badly for him. Hasbro sniffed interestedly at a leg bone, but Perry told him to leave it alone.

The tunnel gate swung slowly open now. It had never been locked at all, really. It was Patrick Cotter that had kept it shut. Patrick Cotter himself had been the skeleton key.

Chapter 22

In the Realm of the Sleeper

Lala shut the gate behind us and tried to make it stay, but it swung open again on its hinges. By opening it for ourselves, we had opened it for everyone, including our enemies, and by starting up Patrick Cotter, we had ended him. At that moment we all heard a fierce banging on the boathouse door above. Without a word we ran, including Hasbro, and like Mr. Boskins, we didn't look back. We ran and we ran and we ran, with Brendan in the lead, holding out the lantern as steadily as he could, and all the time we were going downward, deeper and deeper into the earth until I began to wonder where exactly we were running to and how long we could keep it up.

Finally we slowed down and began to catch our breath, but we kept walking fast, and it was some time before any of us could talk. The wet and weedy smell of the lake and of damp stone had long faded, and instead there was a dry, cold, dusty smell. There was no sound yet of anyone following—no running feet and no light behind us. But they were back there somewhere, and they weren't going to go away. They would follow us if ever they could, and the only thing to do was to keep moving and hope they fell far enough behind and got lost.

"I wonder if there's bats," Brendan said.

And Lala said, "There's no bats in the Sleeper's belfry," and then laughed, but none of the rest of us got the joke, and it was just as well, as it turned out, because we caught on soon enough, when it was too late to turn back.

We had walked, it seemed, for ever so long, when Brendan said that his arm was tired from holding up the lantern, and so Lala took it and we went on again, although not hurrying now, but pacing ourselves. Perry had the can of lamp oil, and I took that, just to keep things fair. After a time there was a fork in the tunnel, one heading downward and one going along straight. Lala stopped for a moment and thought about it, and I could hear her sort of murmuring to herself, although not in any language I could understand, and then we were away again, along the downward fork.

"We might need a rhyme," Lala said suddenly. It sounded meaningless to me. A rhyme?

"What sort of rhyme?" Perry asked. "Like 'Simple Simon'?"

"Or 'Kits cats sacks and wives'?" Brendan asked.

"I think 'Humpty Dumpty' should do the trick," Lala said. "If we all have the same rhyme we could say it together."

"What trick is that?" I asked.

"To keep our minds occupied, should they need it. Sometimes words get going around in your head and don't let other things in. A rhyme is like a charm."

"What 'other things'?" I asked, but she didn't answer. I had no idea of *needing* a rhyme to keep my mind occupied, but I recited "Humpty Dumpty" to myself anyway, just to keep the rhyme within easy reach. I forgot about it, though, when we saw something glowing ahead, a glow like a lantern through fog, and at once I thought of Frosticos and the Creeper, but it couldn't be them. The tunnel opened onto a big, subterranean grotto, stretching away upward and outward so that you couldn't see its end. Not too far ahead of us, partly blocking the path, was a pool of water within a low rock circle.

"Just keep walking," Lala said. And I heard her reciting "Humpty Dumpty" under her breath. Brendan and Perry started to say it, too, but I didn't. I got distracted when I realized that the pool was exactly like the one within the hedge maze, exactly like it, except that there were no waterweeds here, just still, clear water with no bottom. I saw that the glowing light seemed to come from deep within the pool itself, and I paused to look down into it. The others moved on, I guess, although I didn't know. I had forgotten all about them. After a moment of staring, I saw what looked like the small dark shapes of fishes swimming far, far below.

It seemed to me that I could see forever downward, and I gazed deep into it and...lost myself in it, I guess you could say. By and by (I don't know how long) I saw that one of the fish was growing slowly larger, as if it was swimming upward. I waited and watched as it rose in lazy circles. After a time it was just below the surface, peering up at me, and with a shock that caught my breath in my throat I saw that it was a mermaid, and not a fish at all. She had the face of my mother. A feeling came over me, just as it had in my dream on the night before Lala arrived. I was filled with sadness and happiness at the same time, and I put my hand into the water, which was blood-warm. In that moment it came to me that perhaps I could slip away beneath the surface of the pool and simply breathe the water in, just like in a dream, and that I could stay there with my mother, where it would be always light and warm....

Then I felt myself being pulled back, so that I sat down hard on the ground. For a moment I had no idea where I was, or that I was anywhere at all. "You nearly fell in!" Brendan said. "You were going over the side!"

"I...know," I said, which must have sounded strange. But I *did* know. I had been about to *let* myself fall in. There was no mermaid now, but only the small fish once again swimming in the depths, unless perhaps they were very large fish, and very much farther away. Perry and Brendan hauled me back when they saw that I didn't want to leave. I knew that it would do no good to tell what I had seen, although Lala was looking at me as if she suspected.

"That's why you want the rhyme," she said. "We'll all want it before we're done."

We hurried on our way again, out of the grotto and into another tunnel, and we didn't slow down until Hasbro growled as if to warn us of something. We stood in silence then and listened, and we could plainly hear the sound of footfalls echoing out of the tunnel behind us. Then there were voices—voices that might have been a great distance away or very close, because sound travels strangely underground. There was no doubt at all, though, that it was Frosticos and the Creeper, and so we were off again, running quietly, and we kept on running until we reached a triple turning in the tunnel and had to stop again to figure out the way.

Almost at once we saw a light in front of us, a long way off down the center tunnel, what looked like lantern light. Just like last time, it couldn't be Frosticos and the Creeper, because they couldn't have gotten past us. The light flickered and was abruptly closer, as if it had moved fifty feet in that instant of flickering. It shone on someone, too—someone walking. It was Cardigan Peach, holding the lantern out before him, just as we had seen him doing earlier that very day, or perhaps yesterday now. His black cloak and coat and trousers were almost invisible against the darkness, so he appeared to be a floating head.

"It's old Peach!" Perry whispered.

"Good old Peach!" Brendan put in. "He's out patrolling!"

"It's not him," Lala said. "Not really. He's gone to bed hours ago. It's a dream image. He's been wandering these corridors ever since my father descended to the Center and fell asleep. We'll take his route." We set out up the center tunnel, and soon his lantern flickered again, and old Peach stood before us, but looking past us, as if we weren't there at all.

I couldn't help myself. I said, "Hello, Mr. Peach," but of course he said nothing. He simply stood there, as if barring the way. Hasbro stepped toward him sniffing, but his head went right through Mr. Peach's leg, and in that moment Mr. Peach started forward again and passed through Hasbro and then Brendan and the rest of us like a ghost. We watched the glowing lantern move away down the tunnel, floating along. It flickered again and was gone.

We walked on in silence, the path angling ever downward. Other tunnels opened onto our own, all of them leading away in random directions, some upward and some down. Some were choked with rocks, as if the ceilings had fallen in, and some of them revealed open, empty pits that were murmuring vague noises and what sounded like breathing. Sometimes I could hear voices or laughter, but always from very far away. Some of the voices were familiar, as if I was hearing them inside my own memory, and I recited Humpty Dumpty continuously and stayed carefully to the middle of our own tunnel, not going near the open pits.

After a time it came to me that I could see beyond our circle of lantern light. There was a sort of twilight ahead of us, like being outdoors on a moonlit night, except there wasn't any moon. We had entered another vast cavern, with stalactites and stalagmites towering away either side, and with more visible in the far distance. None of them cast a shadow, and neither did we, as if the light were imaginary. I was just about to point this out when Brendan said, "Listen!"

I heard a noise like wind blowing through tree branches, a swishing and rustling, and then the sound of someone talking—not like the murmuring from the pits in the ground, but real human speech. It stopped abruptly, and there was a dead silence, and we all held our breath listening, and in the silence a voice said, "Bear left," quite clearly. Then another voice said, "I tell you we took the wrong turning." I had heard the Creeper speak maybe three sentences in my whole life, but I would never forget his voice, and it was him who had spoken last.

"We're in the Whispering Gallery," Lala said, with her hands cupped over her mouth so that the sound of her voice couldn't fly away into the emptiness. "They might be very close or they might be far away. Sound carries in the Whispering Gallery." She put her finger to her lips, and we nodded, and started forward again, moving as soundlessly as we could. The windy swishing continued, with now and then a clearly uttered sentence or the distinct sound of footfalls. Sometimes it sounded as if it came from ahead of us, sometimes from behind us.

Then in an otherwise silent moment, Perry coughed, and we all stopped dead still and held our breath. We heard a woman's voice this time—Ms Peckworthy, no doubt—saying, "What's that?" very sharply, as if frightened.

"It's them!" said the Creeper's voice.

We heard the scuffling of feet, distinctly now, very close, and Ms Peckworthy's voice saying, "Don't leave me behind!" And then the Creeper saying, "Don't be a-clinging to me!" Then a light appeared, bobbing in the darkness, far away to our left—how far we couldn't tell—and three dark figures were moving in the light.

"Krikey!" Perry said. "He's got an elephant rifle!"

I didn't know about the elephant part, but the Creeper had a rifle, right enough—an immense thing, slung over his shoulder. If we could see them, then of course they could see us. Instantly we were running again, deeper into the earth, and never mind the noise.

Chapter 23

The Darkness of Sleep

The sound of our own feet echoed around us, magnifying itself so that it sounded as if dozens of people were running, the sound rising in volume, the echoes stacking up on top of each other until there was a sort of landslide of noise. Then it stopped, and there was only the normal sound of our own running. We had left the Whispering Gallery behind, and were in a tunnel again, with another triple turning ahead. Lala led us straight into the center tunnel, with us following blindly, until we were too tired to run any farther. I had completely lost track of time and distance. I couldn't say whether we had walked two miles or ten, and that began to trouble me, and questions began to come into my mind. "Where's your father sleeping?" I asked Lala. "Is there a *room* down here?"

"A room? There might be any number of rooms," Lala said, "but there's no bedroom, if that's what you mean—more like a sort of cave, and not till we get to the center."

"What *center* would that be?" I asked.

"The land at the center of the Earth," she said. "Didn't you know that?"

"Look here, Peach," Perry said to her. "What Perkins is asking is *how far do we have to go?* I mean..."

"All the way to the *center*," she replied. "Just like I said. It's neither far nor near."

Lala has her own special way of answering and yet not answering, which can make me impatient.

"You mean to *Pellucidar*?" Brendan put in. "Like in the books?"

"If you'd like," she told him.

"I'd like that very much," Brendan said.

"I mean, if you'd like to *call* it that. That's what my father calls it."

"I'm rather confused," I said in my pleasantest voice. "We're on our way to wake up your father...?"

"To *not* wake him up," Lala said. "To make sure he *doesn't* wake up. And we've got to hurry. We don't want him waking up before we get there, you see."

"If you mean get to the center of the *Earth*," I said, "then I don't see. I can't believe we're going to get there at all. It's 3,959 miles to the center of the Earth. We might as well try to walk to Africa."

"But we don't have any reason to walk to Africa," Lala said.

"If the Earth is *hollow*," Brendan put in, "then we're not going to the *center* center anyway, Perkins. We're going to the outside of the inside, which can't be nearly so far."

"Or the inside of the outside," Lala said, "depending."

"That's right," Brendan said. "Depending."

"Still, that's a mighty fur piece," Perry put in. "Calculate it for us, Perkins."

I tried to figure it out as we walked along, using pi, but I couldn't be sure, because of course we couldn't know for certain the diameter of the interior world, although Admiral Byrd guessed that it was about 4,000 miles across when he flew down into it. That would take up nearly half the diameter of the Earth itself, and yet it would still be two thousand miles beneath our feet, although there was the atmosphere to think about. But even if there were a thousand miles of atmosphere, and we didn't have nearly so far to go, it would still take us weeks or months of walking to get there. If you dug a well to the very center of the Earth and dropped a stone down the well, it would take forty-five minutes to fall. We weren't falling down a well, we were walking down a tunnel, and although the tunnel was sloping downward, it was only just barely. Probably it would be *easier* to walk to Africa.

"It's impossible," I said. "Even if we were climbing straight down a ladder we would starve to death on the way. It's too far."

And it was true. We hadn't brought any food. We hadn't brought any water, only a can of lamp oil. Unless there was something that we didn't know, it was a fool's errand that we were on. And now when I thought of food, I thought of the dinner I hadn't eaten, and suddenly I was hungry and thirsty and wished I hadn't thought about it at all. The St. George Lodge seemed ever so far away, and Mrs. Wattsbury's roast pork and potatoes and applesauce was a feast that I had squandered hours and hours ago. It would have been better to feed it to the hedgehogs, like Brendan did.

"It's all relative anyway," Lala said.

"Relative to *what*?" I asked, for how could distance be relative in any way that made a difference to us?

"Relative to *who*, you mean," Lala said.

"Perkins means relative to *whom*, actually," Perry said, in the voice of the ugly grammar devil that often inhabits his mind.

"We've entered the realm of the Sleeper, now," Lala said. "All the whoms in the world can't change that. Only the Sleeper can change things now. Everything is relative to him, don't you see? And we'd best hope he doesn't change things very much, at least not while we're in the Passage."

I still most certainly did not see, and I was just about to say so when the tunnel opened up into another grotto. It was impossible to say how large, because the lantern didn't make enough light to illuminate it. But there was a sound like wind blowing through open spaces, and it *felt* perfectly immense. The trail, if that's what you'd call it, was still clear, running out ahead of us, like a dark ribbon of stone laid into the floor, and I was anxious to follow it to the other side of the grotto, because the open darkness surrounding us seemed to be full of invisible things—a room full of memories all swirling around like restless ghosts. It sounds weird, but I can't say it any more clearly than that.

High above us in the darkness now there were tiny flashes of light, little on-and-off twinkles like thousands of matches being struck and then immediately going out. Brendan said, "Fireflies," but that didn't sound likely, not this far underground. I remembered a film about the human brain that we had seen in science class. It showed nerve cells turning on and off with little flashes of light deep inside someone's head, like electric sparks. Right then the nerve cells in my own brain started firing like crazy. I thought about Cardigan Peach out rowing on the lake and wandering through the tunnels when in fact he was not doing either of those things, and I thought about what we had seen out over the ocean when we were with Lala in the sea cave. I thought about bats in the belfry and the strange business of the Sleeper growing restless or waking up too soon. I thought about seeing my mother in the pool, when of course she couldn't have been there, and I knew then that it must have been a *memory* of my mother, swimming up from the depths of my own mind.

And now we were passing through this vast room full of memories, or maybe dreams, all of them flitting around us like bats, and I knew that Lala hadn't been talking nonsense at all. It *wasn't* thousands of miles to the center of the Earth, not by the route we were taking. It couldn't be measured in miles, which was just what she had meant when she said it was "relative." And it was what Captain Sodbury had meant when he said what he said about being able to "participate" in the mind projections. He had thought it was nonsense, but it wasn't. Suddenly I felt as if I were nowhere and no-when, but was traveling through the darkness of outer space. Or, I thought, through the darkness of sleep.

A light blinked on now, exactly as if someone had flipped a switch. We weren't in a cavern, but more like a real room in a house or in a museum. It was vastly high, full of ancient wooden furniture. There was an immense clutter of it, piled helter-skelter. There were chairs and tables and dressers and big wardrobe cabinets and beds and grandfather clocks, all of it heaped up, piece upon piece, all the way to the distant ceiling. The walls were covered with strange wallpaper, with odd designs in colors that were deep but faded, like old bloodstains or autumn leaves.

A human figure had appeared in among the furniture now, or else he had always been there but I hadn't seen him. He was creeping and crawling along, high up, near the ceiling. He wore a nightshirt and nightcap, and his hair stuck out from under the nightcap in a wild way. There was a sort of panic in the air now, and I could feel fear rising in my throat, like the moment before you awaken from a nightmare, and your heart is going like crazy and you can barely breathe.

The figure climbed across tabletops on his hands and knees. He crept monkey-like across chairs, up and over the backs of old sofas and in behind wardrobes, disappearing among the shadows and then reappearing farther on, sometimes coming to a dead end and then turning and going back, sometimes pulling himself through very narrow spaces, clearly trying to make his way to the floor, although he didn't quite seem to know the way, only that he meant to climb deeper and deeper until he reached it.

"Keep *walking*," Lala whispered. She was looking downward, unhappily. *It's Giles Peach*, I thought. *Lala's father!* As we walked, we seemed to be drawing the room along with us, as if we were part of the dream, and couldn't simply leave. The nameless fear was rising in me, like water filling up a bucket. I could smell the dusty furniture and feel the hard surface of tables against my knees, and I began to feel as if I myself were high overhead, looking down on all of us below. I saw an age-dark, wooden wardrobe closet just ahead of me, with its door gaping open, and it came into my mind that if I crawled into the darkness of that closet I might find a secret entrance through its floor, and make my way downwards, deeper and deeper into the dim clutter of furniture below.

"Humpty Dumpty sat on the wall," Lala said softly into my ear. "*Say it.* Say it until I tell you it's safe to stop. Say it *now.*"

And so I said it, over and over, and by saying it the spell was broken, and I was myself again, and the room with its furniture and crawling man winked away, and was gone in the darkness.

"*Don't stop*," Lala said, and so all of us kept on murmuring the rhyme as we walked, letting the words go round and round in our heads, filling it up so that other things were kept out.

We passed other rooms, if you could call them that, which you can't, really. I knew now that they were dreams—the Sleeper's dreams—and not rooms at all. The realm of the Sleeper was the sleeping mind of Giles Peach, and the creeping figure had been Peach himself, or his sleeping self, crawling through the cluttered landscape of a dream. We saw him again on a grass-covered meadow with a clear stream running through it. That time there was no fear in the air, but something wonderful instead, almost like a song, which I could feel even though I was still reciting "Humpty Dumpty." And still I didn't stop with the rhyme, and when Brendan and Hasbro walked out onto the meadow, Lala and I grabbed them and pulled them back. We saw Lala's father again on a road that stretched away toward rocky desert hills. He was leading a camel by a rope and was dressed in robes, like a figure from the bible. Then we saw him flying a bamboo airplane over the tops of forest trees, just like what we had seen when we were in the sea cave.

Then we were in a tunnel again, and the dreams were behind us. Far ahead of us a glowing disk of light hovered in the air. At first I thought it was Cardigan Peach's lantern. But it held steady, not like someone walking with a lamp. It was bright and intense—sunlight shining through a cave mouth! I could suddenly smell outside air, and for the first time since leaving Patrick Cotter behind I felt as if I were in a real tunnel and not a dream tunnel.

Hasbro barked and ran toward the daylight, and Brendan started after him, and we were all running then, on and on. Just when it seemed to me that I had to stop to rest or else fall over with exhaustion, we found ourselves at the sunlit cave mouth, looking out over the interior world from halfway up a steep mountain. Perry blew out the lamp, and Hasbro barked again, and we were there!

The wind blew toward us, up from the distant valley floor, carrying on it the smell of flowers and jungle. In the distance away to our right, perhaps a couple of miles away, lay the waters of the interior sea along a rocky shore, and way off to our left stood a steep, dark range of misty cliffs, covered with dense jungles that crept down from the upper slopes. Smoke rose lazily from a volcano even farther off, and ranges of mountains rose beyond that. Overhead the misty glow of the interior sun shone in a blue sky, a sun that never set. There was perpetual daylight in the interior world. It might have been noon and it might have been midnight. I had no idea of time having passed at all in the tunnels, except something like time in a dream, which can seem to go on forever, but really only takes moments.

For a while none of us moved, but only stood and gaped, breathing the air of the land that time forgot.

Then Lala said, "We've got to go back."

Chapter 24

Savage Pellucidar

"You're bonkers, Peach," Perry said to her.

She shook her head. "We made a wrong turn. We must have."

"But we're *here*," Brendan told her, gesturing toward the jungle below us, its trees hundreds of feet tall.

"We're *not* here," she said, "not where we're supposed to be."

I took out my camera and turned it on, and Lala looked at it and then at me in a sort of poisonous way, as if I'd just thrown trash all over the ground. But before I could say anything at all a pterodactyl flew out of a clearing below, rising up into the hazy blue sky and winging away over the forest toward the distant cliffs. It had a great long beak and little claws on its wings—wings that stretched twenty feet or more. Hasbro barked at it, as if even he was surprised to see it. Of course I zoomed my camera out and snapped a picture of it. I had my first real photo of a living dinosaur—*the* first real photo of a living dinosaur!

"Perkins!" Perry hollered at me, and I turned around to see that Lala was gone. She had bolted back into the cave. Our guide had deserted us! Brendan held a match to the lantern, and we plunged back into the darkness, hurrying to catch up with her. There had been a confusion of tunnels only a short way back, which was no doubt where she was bound, and once she got there, if she chose a different tunnel and simply went on without us, we would have no idea which tunnel she had taken. She doesn't need us anymore, I thought—she doesn't even need the lantern—and I was suddenly scared and angry both.

Before we had traveled fifty steps back into the tunnel, a light shone in the distance, just the tiniest glow. We stopped where we were and covered our own lamp with a jacket, and Brendan said, "Maybe it's Cardigan Peach!" in a hopeful voice. For a moment I thought—or hoped—that maybe it was, but before we could start forward again, we heard running footsteps. Perry uncovered the lantern, and Lala burst into our circle of light, bowling right through us, heading back out toward the sunlight. "It's them!" she shouted. "They're after us!" Hasbro, being perhaps the most intelligent among us, turned and ran.

The distant lantern light was jogging along toward us now. It wasn't Cardigan Peach. It was Frosticos and the Creeper and no doubt Ms Peckworthy, too. They had obviously taken the same wrong turn that we had. We followed Lala and Hasbro, straight back out of the cave mouth, but this time we didn't stop to sightsee, but slipped and slid down a sandy little trail until we came upon a tumble of immense boulders nearly blocking the path. We picked our way around them, out of sight of the cave mouth now and at the edge of a plateau covered with a forest of giant tree ferns. Lala left the trail, waving for us to follow, into the shadows of the ferns.

There were chattering noises and birdcalls, but there was an unearthly silence, too—a sort of emptiness in the afternoon air, if it *was* the afternoon. The ground was moss covered, and our footfalls made almost no noise as we moved single file along a narrow game trail, me coming along last beneath a canopy of immense, drooping leaves. There were moving glints of sunlight on the moss as the breeze shifted the leaves overhead. Hasbro started growling, and off to our right a creature the size of an enormous pig, but with a long snout, moved away into the undergrowth, disappearing into the shadows. I snapped a quick picture of it, which I knew would show almost nothing more than the back end of a pig. Almost as soon as the pig creature disappeared, three bright blue birds with enormously long tail feathers flew past low overhead with a rush of beating wings, and I snapped their picture, too, hoping there was enough sunlight for the color to come through.

The trail went upward for a time and then downward again. We seemed to be circling the mountain, roughly in the direction of the inland sea, but I wasn't paying any real attention, because there was too much to look at, and I kept imagining Mr. Collier's face when he saw my photo diary. The only problem was that the pterodactyl had been so far away that it might be mistaken for a pelican, and the blue birds were beautiful, but they weren't evidence, if you see what I mean. Part of me wanted to see something *really* amazing—a triceratops, maybe, or a saber-toothed tiger—but part of me didn't want to see any such thing, because I wasn't anxious to be eaten or trampled. I got a picture of a line of six snails in long spiral shells, moving along in single file. They were almost as large as Reginald Peach's water helmet, and they were the most beautiful tiger-striped brown and gold. But would they look like giants to someone who was seeing the photo for the first time, or like a picture of six small aquarium snails taken close up? I called Brendan's name, hoping to get him to crouch down by the snails, but Brendan was gone, and I had to run to catch up.

Brendan said something sharp to me about lollygagging, but before I could think of a reply we were interrupted by the sound of an explosion, followed by two more.

"Gunfire!" Perry said.

Brendan nodded. "The elephant rifle!"

"They're too *close*," Lala said. "They're tracking us!"

She had a look of intense loathing and anger on her face as well as fear, and I was reminded of the way she had looked at my camera back at the mouth of the cave. The sound of the rifle was simply wrong, if you understand what I mean—the sound of ruination. It was out of place in Pellucidar. Had the Creeper *killed* something? Would it be the first of many things that would die now that the two of them had arrived? Then it came to me that except for Lala, all of us were interlopers, and I wondered whether this was actually the beginning of the end of Pellucidar.

There was the sound of another rifle shot, and I said, "I'm afraid of the Creeper," without really thinking.

"It's not him that you should fear," Lala said after a moment. "It's the other one."

I already knew that, and I didn't really want to think about it. "Why are they tracking us?" I asked. "They're already here. Isn't that what they wanted? He said that they needed you down in the Passage. We're not in the Passage now."

"They want something...more," she said, but she was already turning away, and we were moving on, as fast as ever, forced to climb upward again by a high wall of dark, volcanic rock, and then downward again through a steep little canyon that twisted and turned until I had no idea whether we were going in any sensible direction or were just wandering. Lala pressed on, though, as if she knew exactly where we were going.

It seemed to me that we were running away from something and toward something both, but why? "What do they *want*?" I said, sort of gasping the question out.

She surprised me by stopping again and turning around. "They want to kill my father," she said. The Lala who talked in riddles and half answers had suddenly turned into the Lala who was deadly serious.

The three of us stood blinking at her. "But why?" I asked. "Why would they do that?"

"Because they don't want him to wake up. Ever. They want the Passage to be frozen open. If a Sleeper dies in the middle of a dream, the dream doesn't die. It's suspended, floating there like a soap bubble for years. They want to be able to come and go through the passage. They want this to be theirs." She gestured with her hand, taking in all of Pellucidar. "They'll exploit it and spoil it and kill things and take things away, and everything that it is will pass away. Forever. There would be no bringing it back."

"So this has happened before?" Perry asked shrewdly. "The death of a Sleeper? That's how you know?"

"Yes," she said, turning and moving on again, talking over her shoulder. "Two hundred years ago. The Sleeper was Eulalie Peach, my grandmother ten generations back. I'm named after her. She was a mermaid and she was born here. It's her in the glass casket that was in the museum. The Passage remained open for years after she died in her sleep, although it was very dangerous to traverse, because the lingering dreams could drive you mad and because portions of it kept collapsing. People tried to get through it, though, and it had to be guarded day and night. When the Passage finally closed again the skeleton gate was devised to lock it off, and the key was hidden in the casket."

"Now Frosticos is going to make it happen again," Brendan said.

"*Make* it happen, yes. Before the moon is full, and that's soon. Very soon. That's why they're in a hurry."

"So we can't wake him up and we can't let him sleep," Perry said.

"Yes," she said, and then, "no," and that was the end of the conversation.

We came out of the canyon into a jungle, with vines and cascades of flowers hanging from the trees, which towered away overhead. There were birds moving through the trees and what must have been monkeys, although they were hidden in shadow. We could hear them chittering away and see branches moving. Immense butterflies fluttered overhead. The ground was completely shaded, too shady for underbrush, but with mosses and ferns and gigantic orchids growing from the tree trunks. In the distance, through the trees, lay a big meadow, knee deep in grass and wildflowers. And on the meadow, like figures in a diorama in a natural history museum, stood half a dozen wooly mammoths, perfectly enormous and shaggy, with long, bent tusks. They were twice the size of African elephants—as big as houses.

Perry said, "Krikey," again, which pretty much expressed what we were all thinking, and I forgot everything else and crept nearer to the tree line to get a clearer picture—thinking that even Mr. Collier couldn't argue with a wooly mammoth, something that no living human being on the surface of the earth had seen. I got off exactly two pictures before Lala had already disappeared, and we had to go on again or be left behind. We weren't important to Lala, and neither was a herd of mammoths. Nothing could be more important to Lala than saving her father's life, and saving her father's life meant saving Pellucidar from the likes of Frosticos and the Creeper. And if the Sleeper woke up in the meantime, we'd all be in trouble. Trouble, I mean to say, loomed on every side.

We moved away downhill now, toward the edge of the sea, the ground getting rockier and the smell of salt in the air instead of rotting vegetation. It was suddenly cooler, too, when we came out of the trees onto a long, rocky shelf, full of tide pools. Waves washed across the pools, and crabs the size of car tires scuttled around on the rocks waving giant pincers, disappearing down into crevasses and walking out into the ocean. Sea birds no different from our own sea birds flew through the air, swooping down into the water after fish. The wind blew off the sea, straight into us now that we were out of the shelter of the jungle.

We crossed the rocks and jumped down onto a stretch of hard-packed sand. House-sized rocks stood up out of the sea like a half circle of islands, blocking the waves and wind and creating a sort of bay. The shallow water along the edge of the bay was a golden-blue, like the sky, but only a few feet from shore it was a deeper blue, shading to black. The surface of the bay seemed to be roiled up, as if something big was swimming right under the water, or maybe a lot of somethings—a dense school of fish, maybe.

Lala stood some distance ahead now, looking into a little clearing at the edge of the sand. Brendan and Hasbro ran on ahead to catch up with her, but she didn't wait. She went on up into the trees again. The jungle grew almost down to the shore there, and at the edge of the jungle, in that clearing, someone had built a driftwood hut. Pieces of driftwood formed the skeleton frame of a roof, tied together with long shreds of leaf, although much of it had been blown to pieces or rotted away. There were fern and palm leaves tied to the top to keep the rain out.

On the ground in front of the hut stood a ring of stones from a campfire. Burned driftwood and ashes lay within the ring, half covered in sand. One of the rocks had been moved into the shelter of the hut itself—a flat, circular stone, the bottom black from the fire, and on the top of the stone someone had very neatly written her initials in charcoal. I say "her" because the initials were "A. W. P."—Abigail Wallace Perkins, my mother. I stood staring at it. I didn't need any other proof that it had been her. Who else could it have been? She had been looking for a passage to the interior world, and she had found it. She hadn't drowned in the depths of the Sargasso Sea. She had descended beneath it.

"Perkins," Perry said softly, and nodded up toward the jungle. Half hidden by vegetation that had grown up around it lay a big glass sphere, maybe seven feet in diameter, banded with metal rings. It was my mother's bathyscaph. I had seen a picture of it once, standing on bent legs with arms for reaching and grappling things, and with my mother standing next to it, smiling. But the legs were broken off now and were nowhere to be seen. A piece of one of the arms was still attached to the sphere, snapped off and twisted out of shape. One of the heavy glass panes was shattered.

My mother was alive. She had found the submarine passage somewhere deep in the Sargasso and had gotten through it in the bathyscaph. She had bobbed to the surface of the interior ocean and floated ashore. She had built a hut on the beach, made a fire, rolled the wrecked bathyscaph up onto dry land, and...what?

Walked away? To where? There were no footprints, no arrows carved into tree trunks, nothing but four thousand miles of a wide, empty, primeval world. Could she have survived at all, alone in this world? What had wrecked the bathyscaph? What terrors had she faced here, alone on the beach? I took a picture of the bathyscaph. It would mean nothing to Mr. Collier, but everything to Uncle Hedge. To me it meant hope.

"Holy moly," Brendan said, very softly.

"Yeah," I said, not really listening.

"What *is* it?" Perry whispered. "*Perkins!*"

They were staring at the bay, at the moving water. A black, humped shape was cutting through it now. It was vast, the size of a whale, and abruptly it disappeared beneath the surface. It had to have been thirty or forty feet long, perfectly enormous. I raised my camera very slowly in case it came back up. But all was still, and we stood there holding our breath, looking at nothing at all.

And then the water simply exploded, like a bomb had gone off. "Zeuglodon!" I shouted, as the creature threw itself into the air, its great, angular head rising twenty and then thirty feet, its mouth open, showing rows of triangular teeth. Its black, glittering eye looked small in that enormous head, but must have been the size of a grapefruit.

I snapped a picture at the same time that I was turning to run, and I saw the creature slam back down again, thrashing around toward us. I realized that I was screaming now, as a wall of water washed across the beach, knocking down the driftwood hut and carrying it up into the jungle.

We kept running even though we knew that the zeuglodon was an ocean-going reptile and that we were safe from it. We were angling uphill, running blindly toward a bend in the trail ahead, thinking only about catching up with Lala, with not being left behind, when out from the shadows of the trees stepped the Creeper, grinning a snaggle-toothed grin and holding the elephant rifle in his hands, blocking the path. I heard Perry shout a useless warning, and I stopped cold, but Brendan slammed into my back and we both fell over in a heap. When I scrambled back up to my feet, there was nowhere to run.

Chapter 25

The Third Arrival
of Ms Peckworthy

"What have we here?" the Creeper asked, as if he was really curious. "It's the three little scally-wags, or I'm a Dutchman!" There was a noise behind us, and I turned to see Dr. Frosticos staring at us, although with no real interest, as if we were a plate of yesterday's food and he wasn't hungry. His eyes were simply cold. Compared to him the Creeper seemed to be made of cardboard.

"Hello, pillbug," the Creeper said to me now in a smarmy voice. "Finally I've a chance to thank you for throwing that ring-a-ding to me. Because of that we meet again in this lovely place!"

"Bind them," Frosticos said in a flat voice. "To the tree there. Be quick about it. The Peach girl has apparently gone on ahead."

The Creeper set the big rifle against a low tree limb and then drew a coil of rope out of a canvas pack. He made a slip-loop in the end of it, then grabbed Brendan by the shoulder and spun him around, wrenching his hand behind his back and tying his wrists. "You next," he said to Perry. But he must have seen something in Perry's face, because he said, "Don't even *think* about any of your billy-club capers, young bunion. There's no one to help you here. Your dear old uncle is as dead as a pickled herring. They'll have him on ice by now, I should think."

"Liar!" Brendan shouted at him.

The Creeper shook his head sadly. "Quite dead, I'm afraid. He put up a gallant struggle, but in the end his blood was as red as the next man's, as the quaint old saying goes."

"Then who's *that*," Perry said, pointing farther along the path. The Creeper and Frosticos both looked, and so did I— looked at nothing, because the path was empty—and in that moment who should step silently out from among the trees behind us but Ms Peckworthy, still carrying her umbrella, although it was nothing but ribs and tatters now. Perry had seen her, and she must have given him a sign, although what she thought she was up to I didn't know.

The Creeper looked back now and saw her. He stood staring for a moment before he started to speak, which was a big mistake, because she very calmly flung the umbrella in his face like a spear at the same moment that she bent forward and snatched up the elephant rifle, which must have weighed nearly as much as she did.

"Poppycock!" she said, hoisting the rifle to her shoulder and looking at the Creeper in a deadly way, as if she'd had enough of him. It dawned on me with a wild gladness that Ms Peckworthy was one of us, and not our nemesis at all. Her arrival last night on the Manchester bus had been one of the worst things in my life, but her arrival here in the middle of the jungle was one of the best.

"Be careful now, my good woman..." the Creeper started to say, and he took a cautious step toward her, waving both hands in front of himself as if trying to reason with her. The rifle went off right then, the explosion so loud that my ears rang. I sprang back, covering my face, and when I opened my eyes I saw that the Creeper had thrown himself to the ground. At first I thought he had been shot, but the rifle was pointed skyward. Ms Peckworthy lowered it again, still glaring at him. Dr. Frosticos stood there like an ice sculpture, staring right through her, simply biding his time.

"My father taught me to shoot when I was a girl," Ms Peckworthy said, narrowing her eyes. "In the Michigan woods. I never thought I'd put the talent to use."

In that moment the Creeper lunged forward, snatching at the barrel of the rifle, but Perry stuck his foot out and tripped him, so neatly that it looked like judo or something, and the Creeper sprawled forward in the dirt again as Ms Peckworthy backed off a step.

"You detestable skunks!" she said to both of them. "You oily cretins! You unnatural crocodiles!" She stared down the barrel of the rifle, letting the Creeper writhe in his own slime for a moment. Then to Perry she said, "Untie your brother and then tie these two pieces of human detritus up tightly." And then to the Creeper: "You! Put your hands together and hold them out in front of you, where the boy can get a rope on them. You too, Doctor, if you *are* a doctor and not a miserable fraud." She pointed the rifle straight at Frosticos now. She had a wild gleam in her eye, as if she had been waiting for just this moment, and was relishing it.

"You wouldn't leave us here?" the Creeper said, making his sad face. "Tied up like a Sunday roast? You saw that great bear near the cave!"

"You'd leave the children here, wouldn't you?...you...you prevaricating gudgeon! When that bear reared up from the rocks, you scuttled off thinking it would eat *me*, and it very nearly did! You two can sit here until doomsday and consider your evil ways as far as I'm concerned, and if a bear bites either of your heads off...too bad for the bear!"

Too much talking, I thought. *We're burning daylight.*

What happened next was a surprise. Dr. Frosticos took a long look at the Creeper, shook his head dismissively, and then turned around and walked calmly away down the path like a man who had seen enough and was going back to the hotel, so to speak. In about three seconds he was out of sight. There was nothing to be done. Ms Peckworthy wasn't going to shoot anyone. Frosticos knew it, and we knew it, and by now the Creeper knew it too. But Perry had already looped the slipknot over the Creeper's wrists and tightened it, and now Ms Peckworthy made the Creeper sit down beside the tree that he had been going to tie us to. Brendan and Perry looped the rope around and around him, tying half-hitches now and then, yanking the rope tight each time. "More knots," Ms Peckworthy said. "Make the bear work for his supper!" But the rope was pretty much used up, and the Creeper was tight to the tree.

"Come along, children," she said. We didn't discuss it, but went on up the hill in the direction that Lala must have taken, hurrying, because clearly Frosticos would walk straight back into things as soon as we were gone and untie that rope. Tying up the Creeper might buy us five minutes. If Lala were going to succeed, I thought, she'd best already have found her father and gone on her way. She'd been smart enough to ignore distractions, but I hadn't been.

The trail wound along a steep cliff now, and shortly we came out into a sort of clearing, with dense brush below and a view of the rocky mountainside high above. Without slowing her pace, Ms Peckworthy said, "Stand clear!" and she twirled sideways and let go of the elephant rifle, which spun around and around, sailing out over the cliff and down into the brush, out of sight, where it would lie until forever and rust, and good riddance to it.

We went on, and some minutes later we emerged from the trees again, where we found ourselves at the edge of a stream that was rushing through a narrow little gorge, the water splashing and plunging maybe thirty feet below. There was a footbridge across the stream, the bridge made of jungle vines and broken limbs, the vines tied to tree trunks on either side. The whole thing looked rickety and old.

"That appears to be unsafe," Ms Peckworthy said, shaking her head doubtfully.

But the word meant nothing, because *not* crossing the bridge, and fast, was unsafer by far. Perry stepped boldly out onto it, and then coaxed Ms Peckworthy across. I followed, and Brendan came last. We started up the trail again double-time, and were fifty feet from the bridge before I realized that Brendan wasn't behind me. I turned, and there he was, back at the bridge, sawing away at the vines with the Creeper's knife. I whistled, and he looked up, waved us on, and went back to work. There was no sign of Frosticos and the Creeper, and one side of the bridge already leaned precariously, the vines severed, and so we went on without Brendan, soon coming out of the trees onto a grassy sort of plateau.

The stream we had crossed was bubbling out of a massive tumble of rocks above, pouring down over them in a broad, smoothly-flowing waterfall. It was marshy ground, and Lala's footprints were easy to see, leading away into the rocks. There were other footprints, too—enormous three-toed prints, and prints that might have been from a giant cat. I snapped pictures, aiming with one hand as we hurried onward.

Within moments we stood at the bottom edge of that tumble of rocks. There was a broad view of the sea below, looking quiet and placid, and of the clearing along the trail where Ms Peckworthy had thrown the elephant rifle. There was no sign of Brendan, but most of the trail was hidden from view, and I knew he wouldn't waste a moment once the bridge was cut. We paused long enough to gulp water from a clear pool in the rocks—the first water we'd had since last night. I was thirsty as a desert.

I became aware then of the sound of bees, a *lot* of bees, very close by. This time I knew what the sound meant, and I didn't bother to look for any real bees. We soon discovered that there was an opening behind the waterfall, leading into a cavern very much like our own sea cave, but deeper and darker—so deep and dark that I couldn't see the back of it. The bee noises were coming from inside the cavern, from somewhere in the darkness, and the air smelled of water on stone because of the mist from the waterfall.

I realized that Ms Peckworthy had grasped my wrist and was holding on tightly. "I can't see a *thing* in the dark," she whispered, her voice full of fear. "What is it? What's that noise? I don't like bees, *especially* in the dark."

"It's not bees," I said. "It's the sound of...dreaming."

"Of *dreaming*?" she whispered. "My land! Will wonders never cease?"

"Not for a while yet," I told her.

I could see better now, and I made out something that would have been very strange, except that I was half expecting it. Farther back in the cavern, almost lost in the shadows, stood a big four-poster bed. The posts were apparently cut out of tree trunks, with the bed's four feet carved to look like elephant's feet. Rays of watery light filtering down through the waterfall shone on them and on the headboard, which appeared to be a crown, like a king would wear. A man in a nightshirt and nightcap lay on the bed, asleep atop a cloud-like mattress that must have been stuffed with mounds of feathers.

It was the Sleeper, Giles Peach, Lala's inventive father, who had descended into this cave and fallen asleep when the time was right, like a salmon putting away his daily business in the sea and swimming upriver. Lala stood next to him. She held a finger to her lips to keep us quiet. "I've been trying to get him to walk without awakening him," she whispered, "but he's *very* obstinate."

I was thinking about other obstinate people, like the Creeper and Frosticos, who at this moment were no doubt moving in our direction. I peered out of the mouth of the cave, and thank goodness I saw Brendan climbing the hill. I waved him on, holding my finger to my lips to keep him from blurting anything out. We *really* needed to be gone into the darkness of the Passage and headed for home. With the bridge down we had a chance, a real chance, and we couldn't afford to squander it.

Brendan stood in the cave mouth, trying to see in. "I left him at the bridge," he whispered, breathing hard.

"*Him?*" I asked. "The Creeper?"

"Frosticos. The Creeper wasn't with him. He came alone." He shivered, remembering.

He left the Creeper behind, I thought, realizing the truth. Frosticos didn't need the Creeper now. The Creeper had been merely convenient, like a piece of tissue when your nose needs blowing, and we had tied the used tissue to a tree trunk with about sixty knots. Now he would be dinner, just as he had feared.

I heard Lala mutter something into her father's ear now. She waited a moment and then muttered it again. He stirred in his bed and rolled over onto his side, and then, wonder of wonders, he sat up, swiveled around, and with his eyes still closed, set his feet on the ground. He had a pleasant smile on his face, as if his current dreams were good dreams. Hasbro wandered over and sniffed at him.

"Time!" Lala whispered, and she rummaged under the bed and came up with a pair of bedroom slippers, which she slid onto his feet. He stood up then, with his arms held out in front of him, and set out sleepwalking, straight toward the back of the waterfall. Lala took his elbow and very gently turned him around, and they moved deeper into the cave, where I could see the mouth of the Passage clearly now, leading away into the depths of the mountain.

Chapter 26

When the Sleeper Awakens

We went up the Passage, bound for home, with Lala and her father going on ahead and Brendan and Perry and Hasbro a few paces behind, trying to keep the lantern light from shining into the Sleeper's eyes. Ms Peckworthy and I came along behind them. The bees were quieter now, as if some of them had gone off to work and the hive was emptying out. That worried me, because I didn't know what it meant.

"Is that strange man still *asleep*?" Ms Peckworthy whispered to me.

I said that he was, and that we were sleepwalking him home. And then I told her what I knew, because she had spent most of the last week being confused about almost everything. I told her that the Passage we were in was part of the Sleeper's dream, and that he mustn't wake up, or else the tunnel might go to the place where dreams go when a person awakens, and maybe that's where we'd go too, although we couldn't say for sure where that was, and didn't want to find out. "If I say 'run,'" I told her, "we have to *really* run."

She gripped my arm a little bit tighter, and asked, "How do you know such strange things?"

"I read a lot," I said, and then for a long time we went on in silence, moving along steadily in our little circle of lantern light. I looked back down the tunnel, anticipating the appearance of Dr. Frosticos despite Brendan having cut the bridge loose. I tried to think of how much time it would take him, desperate as he must be, to descend into that gorge, ford the stream, and climb the other side. But that unhappy thought was interrupted by something much worse, although it would have been funny in the light of day.

Hasbro was walking between Lala and the Sleeper now, looking from one to the other as if it was great fun. In a fit of happiness he licked Mr. Peach on the hand, and Mr. Peach said, "Doggy!" just as clear as anything, and very cheerfully.

The sound of his voice speaking out sensibly like that made Lala stop and turn toward him, sort of gaping in fear, and when she did, Perry nearly ran into the back of her. He yanked the lantern sideways so that it wouldn't burn her, and the lantern knocked against the rock wall of the tunnel. The glass broke, oil spilled out, and thank goodness it didn't splatter on anyone, because the oil caught fire, and for the space of thirty seconds the spray of oil on the wall and floor blazed away as light as day, and everybody's horrified faces were frozen in the moment. The Sleeper, thank heavens, didn't open his eyes. The firelight dwindled, faded away entirely, and left us in darkness.

We went on, of course, but even more slowly, the dark pressing down around us like a weight. After a time the Sleeper began to mutter, his voice rising and falling. Mostly he said wild and nonsensical things, but now and then he threw in a phrase that made daytime sense. Clearly he was waking up, but taking his time about it, thank heaven, like a tortoise that's been hibernating. I had one hand out in front of me so that I wouldn't run into Brendan and Perry, and the other on the wall of the tunnel in order to keep straight. Ms Peckworthy held onto a fistful of my jacket and muttered, "Oh my!" and "I just don't *know*!" pretty steadily under her breath. The wild-eyed Ms Peckworthy of the elephant gun caper had disappeared when the lamp went out.

Very slowly there arose around us the sound of creaking and straining and grinding. It was very faint at first, a noise like you'd imagine an earthquake might make, moving deep within the earth, and at first I thought it must be my imagination.

Then I heard Ms Peckworthy whisper, "What's that *noise*?" in a fearful way, and Hasbro growled as if he sensed that something bad was happening. The floor of the Passage began to vibrate ominously, and seemed to tilt, and the sound of moving rock grew louder, then dimmed again and fell silent.

Then a light blinked on in the distance, and Brendan said, "It's old Peach!" just as another rumbling and heaving shook the Passage, nearly throwing us to the ground. It didn't stop this time, but worsened, as dust and rock cascaded down around us.

Lala shouted, "Run!" and we were all running, not blindly now, but toward the light. There was no more keeping quiet. We were running for our lives. We all knew it, just like you know it in a nightmare. I could see the silhouette of the Sleeper a few feet ahead, sort of skipping along, Lala gripping his hand. I hoped he would linger a little longer in his dream, but the thought vanished out of my mind when I realized that there was no longer anyone holding on to my jacket. I had lost Ms Peckworthy! I stopped and turned, but there was only darkness behind. She had let go of me, but when? How far back? If she had shouted out, I hadn't heard her....

I turned and ran back without anyone knowing. If I had shouted to let them know, Brendan and Perry and Hasbro would have followed me, and then there would have been five of us in trouble instead of two. I didn't *want* to go back. I'll tell you that truthfully. Dr. Frosticos was back there somewhere, and the whole Passage was alive with rumbling. I wanted to follow the others toward the light. I wanted to see the sun or the moon, it didn't matter which, and I wanted to be back at the St. George lying in my bed.

But I had to find her. Ms Peckworthy had saved us. She had stuck by us ever since that first day on Mrs. Hoover's front lawn, whether we wanted her to or not. Even the idea of Aunt Ricketts didn't matter—not in that moment.

I groped through the blind darkness, feeling the tremors in the rock, hearing the grinding and shifting again, louder now. There was a shock, like the first jolt of an earthquake, and I fell, tearing the knees out of my jeans. The only thing that would save me or Ms Peckworthy, though, was speed, and so I got up and went on.

Tiny firefly lights began to blink on here and there, as they had when we were entering the room of dreams, but this time they weren't winking out again. It was as if daylight were filling up the Passage. *He's waking up*, I thought, and in that moment I saw Ms Peckworthy, twenty feet farther along, sitting on the floor and holding her head in her hands. She apparently heard my footsteps and looked up, clearly surprised that she could see. "Child!" she started to say, but I said, "No time to talk," and I hauled her to her feet.

"You *shouldn't* have come back!" she moaned as I tried to get her moving. "I was worn out—nothing but a rusty old sea anchor. *Now I've dragged you down with me*. G...g... go on!" she said, "Save yourself! Your Aunt Ricketts would want it! I don't matter!"

"It's Aunt Ricketts that doesn't matter," I told her, angry on Ms Peckworthy's behalf. But it was then that I saw him coming—Dr. Frosticos, running through the darkness. I could scarcely believe it. He seemed to be glowing, too, in the firefly light, as if his ghastly white hair and skin was luminescent. He rushed up the tunnel like a nightmare, his eyes wide, his mouth half open. I screamed and gave Ms Peckworthy a tremendous yank. She suddenly came alive, and within moments she was running like a greyhound, with me behind her now, shouting, "Go! Go!" completely unnecessarily.

I could feel his presence behind me, like a rushing shadow. The ground shook again, hard this time, and both of us lurched sideways, colliding with the wall. There was a terrific grinding noise, and the sound of rocks clattering like boulders tumbling into a canyon. It was the sound of the dream collapsing in on itself.

Suddenly Cardigan Peach appeared forty or fifty feet from us, holding the lantern out before him, showing us the way through a haze of rock dust. We ran toward him, with such a banging and rumbling and grinding in the air that it sounded like the end of the world. I saw Patrick Cotter's gate swinging open ahead, and I saw Perry and Brendan beyond, looking back at us with wild fear on their faces. *Stay!* I shouted, knowing they meant to come to our rescue, but before the shout was uttered, the Passage collapsed behind us with a great, howling, crashing boom that nearly slammed us over.

A dusty wind swept past, and the gate swung on its hinges, and I could smell the weedy, wet smell of the boathouse cellar. Then I saw Patrick Cotter's bones scattered on the stones of the floor and the fallen lock with the key still in it, and Brendan and Perry and Hasbro still staring back toward the Passage. That's when I slowed down and stopped, almost unable to take another step.

There was a silence now, no rumbling or crashing. No sound but our breathing and the quiet splashing of water against the outer wall of the boathouse. Behind us, beyond the open gate, there was no sign of the tunnel, no sign of Dr. Frosticos, only solid rock. The Windermere Passage had closed.

◪

We all went up the stairs together, hearing noises above. A full moon shone through the windows of the boathouse, where Uncle Hedge and Mr. Wattsbury were just coming in through the door, which Lala and her father had opened for them. I was so relieved that I almost laughed out loud. Ms Peckworthy looked like a skinny goblin in her ragged dress, and Giles Peach stood blinking around, still wearing his pointed cloth nightcap and obviously groggy from a long sleep. Lala was hugging him, and he was hugging her, and Hasbro was bounding around as if it had been nothing but a big fat adventure, which is one of the glories of being a dog, because almost everything is.

It was two in morning when we left Lala and Mr. Peach behind after saying our goodbyes. We left Mr. Wattsbury's boat on the beach, not having any gas, and came home in the boat that Mr. Wattsbury and Uncle Hedge had commandeered in order to come after us. A half hour after setting out from the dock at Peach Manor, we sat down around the table at the St. George and ate an early morning breakfast that Mrs. Wattsbury put out for us. This time I *did* eat it, too, with about ten rashers of bacon and a ton of toast and jam. And all the time we were shoving it down we were telling our stories.

There was no sign of the sea anchor in Ms Peckworthy, who joined right in, and said that if it wasn't for me, she would have been left behind and buried in the Passage. She was grateful, she said, and owed me her life, and she meant it, too. We said the same to her, and told Uncle Hedge and the Wattsburies about the elephant rifle, and about the footbridge and what happened to the Creeper. The really funny thing was that Ms Peckworthy realized that she had got caught up in one of Uncle Hedge's shenanigans. Now that she was safe and eating bacon and eggs, it seemed like a very glorious shenanigan to her all the way around.

She went on about how she had followed Mr. Wattsbury through town when he had left for the aquarium, but had lost sight of him near the lake. When she caught up with him again, he was lying on the ground bleeding, and she had gone in through the open door, sure that we were in terrible trouble, and not knowing that Mr. Wattsbury had come to his senses and followed her. She had whacked them and whacked them with her umbrella, she said, as if she couldn't wait to do it all again, cave bear and all. St. George himself would have given her three cheers by the time she was done telling it.

Brendan got up and went upstairs, and when he came back down he shocked us all. He was carrying Ms Peckworthy's notebook! He hadn't burned in the sea cave at all, nor read it either, because he had started feeling ashamed that he had stolen it. He gave it to Ms Peckworthy now and apologized like a gentleman, and she apologized for having underestimated us, and by the end of breakfast we were great good friends, and Ms Peckworthy said that she had been wrong to say that we were troublemakers and layabouts, and that she meant to tell that very thing to Aunt Ricketts and Social Services and anyone else who needed to be told.

What does that go to show you? That people can change, and that they *do* change, sometimes in big ways, which it's easy to forget when you start thinking of someone as your nemesis and forget that you don't really know them at all.

It was nearly dawn when I took out my camera to snap a photo of the whole jolly scene. That led to my looking at the pictures from Pellucidar, and everyone crowding around to see. Mrs. Wattsbury said they were "unbelievable," which they were. The word made me think of Mr. Collier, and how his face would look when I handed in my photographic diary, which would be like nothing he had imagined. I had been worried that the pterodactyl would look like a pelican, but it didn't. It looked like just what it was, soaring through a blue sky with the jungle-clad cliffs beyond. The snails looked perfectly enormous because of the trees and plants behind them, and the wooly mammoths on the meadow didn't appear to be a museum exhibit at all, unless the exhibit was the size of a football field. But the best was the zeuglodon, half out of the water and twisted around toward us, with the ocean and the rocks as a backdrop. Brendan's face was in the bottom of the picture, all wide-eyed and with his mouth open, as if he was looking at his doom.

I had taken only twelve photos in all, but no one who looked at them would have any doubt. The photos would take the "crypto" out of "cryptozoology." The Windermere Passage had closed, but the proof of Pellucidar still resided inside my camera. I sat there thinking about it, happy and tired and full. But as so often happens, one thought led to another, and somehow I began to think about the explosion of that elephant rifle echoing in the distance and the look on Lala's face when she heard it.

The sound of people talking cheerfully filled the room around me, but I wasn't listening now. I was remembering the look that Lala had given me when she first saw my camera outside the mouth of the cave. It came into my mind that a camera could be just like an elephant rifle if you aimed it at the wrong thing and didn't think very hard before you set it off.

I sat there for a time, just thinking. Then I erased the photo of the pterodactyl. Before I could talk myself out of it, I kept on going, sending the mammoths and the snails and the birds and even the zeuglodon back to their rightful home.

Chapter 27

Catching Everything Up

That's nearly the end of my story, and it includes almost absolutely everything that I myself took part in, and that's really the only part I can tell for sure. There are still things you don't know, of course, and so now I'm going to finish with bits and pieces of things. First, what happened to Dr. Frosticos and the Creeper? Was the Creeper eaten alive? Was Frosticos crushed by a collapsing dream? Nobody knows. Brendan said it best when he said, "Good riddance to bad rubbish." What happened during the fight at the aquarium? It ended quickly, mainly because of the Creeper's knife. Ms Peckworthy got taken hostage, and Uncle Hedge and Mr. Wattsbury got locked up behind a barred door. Mrs. Wattsbury had fallen asleep while waiting for Mr. Wattsbury to return, but woke up long past midnight to find that he hadn't. She found the Old Door standing open like we'd left it and then found the two of them and let them out. They made a beeline to Mr. Wattsbury's boat, but of course we had taken it, and so they had to wake up a friend and borrow another boat, and by the time they had tied up at the dock and gotten to the boathouse, there we were. The dust of the adventure had already settled and there was nothing left to do but go back to the St. George and eat.

It sounds impossible, but the only time that had passed for us had been in Pellucidar. Our trek through the Windermere Passage, which had seemed like hours, had been measured in dreamtime.

We stayed in Bowness until the end of spring break, and had more adventures, although they were normal adventures, like finding Betina from the King's Owl and going back down to Peach Manor with her and her old granny. The police were towing the submarine off the shoal when we passed by on the lake, and they took it back up to Bowness and moored it at the dock near the aquarium, where thousands of people flocked down to see it because it was such a marvel.

At the Manor we discovered that Giles Peach had already put Patrick Cotter back together again using what are called cotter pins, and that the giant was back on the job, with the gate locked behind him as ever, even though it's a gate to nowhere, until another Sleeper opens it again. The Mermaid's key and Patrick Cotter's hand are both back in their rightful place in the wonderful South Seas box, which has sadly become the Mermaid's coffin. Old Cardigan Peach took Betty's gran out rowing on the lake, and they took Brendan and Lala along with them. It was a sad, hard thing for Brendan to leave that afternoon. For ten cents and a hot dog he would have stayed forever at Peach Manor, and now he writes Lala postcards nearly every day and positively burns through stamps.

There's only one thing left to tell. A couple of weeks after we returned to Caspar, word came through from Mr.

Wattsbury that the submarine had disappeared from the dock in Lake Windermere. How it had gotten out of the lake was a mystery, but no more of a mystery than how it had gotten into the lake in the first place. The newspaper had reported that it was most likely stolen—craned out of the water in the night and carried away on a flatbed truck. But I wonder about that. What if Dr. Frosticos returned to claim it, and it had resurfaced through the Morecambe Sands and escaped into the sea...?

And now I'm at the end of this book, which I hope has been a good one. Summer is long past. Christmas has come and gone, and in a month it'll be spring again. It's nearly dark outside, and the moon is already up over the ocean. I can hear the bell buoy moaning off the point and the breakers washing in over the rocks in the sea cove.

On the wall of my bedroom I've got two photos that I saved from Pellucidar framed on the wall. One is of a flat rock with three charcoal letters scrawled across it, and the other is of the ruined bathyscaph half overgrown with jungle vegetation.

The sound of the ocean at night always makes me think about my mother, and the moon, which is full tonight, is shining like a lantern in the sky, casting a hopeful light.

The End

Kathleen Perkins
Caspar, California